Lottie Biggs is NOT Desperate

Or
three weeks IN the GrIP
Of a wOmaNLY urGe

this BOOk Is DeDICateD tO

Graham,

mY verY OwN
huNk Of ChuNk.

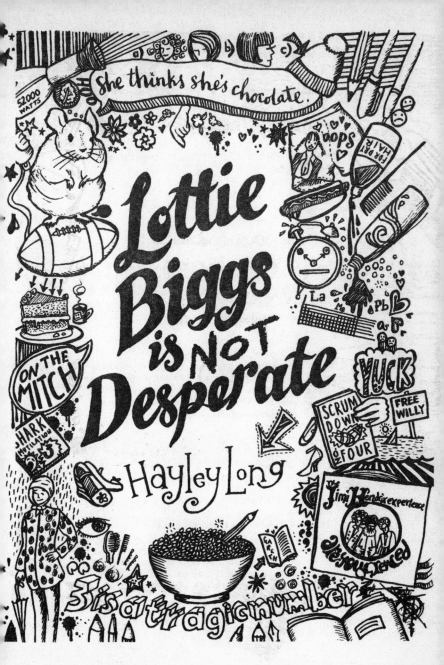

She thinks she's chocolate.

Lottie Biggs is NOT Desperate

Hayley Long

MACMILLAN CHILDREN'S BOOKS

First published 2010 by Macmillan Children's Books
a division of Macmillan Publishers Limited
20 New Wharf Road, London N1 9RR
Basingstoke and Oxford
Associated companies throughout the world
www.panmacmillan.com

ISBN 978-0-330-47975-2

1 3 5 7 9 8 6 4 2

A CIP catalogue record for this book is available from
the British Library.

Printed and bound in the UK by CPI Mackays, Chatham ME5 8TD

CONtemPLatING the COsmIC COmPLeXItIes Of CharLOtte BeYONCé BIGGs

I am an astronaut surfing a wave on the Sea of Tranquillity. I have driven too fast down the motorway to Misery, sailed too far on the sinking ship to Stress and almost lost my head on the bullet train to Oblivion. But now I am gliding gracefully in a positive direction. It won't be a high-speed journey and I must try to be patient and allow myself to float with the cosmic flow. The coastline is getting closer and Chill-out Beach is just in the next bay.

This is the kind of colossal weirdness that Blake comes out with. Blake is from New Zealand and wears flip-flops even when it's raining. Sometimes, the stuff he says is so incredibly cheesy that I have to laugh even if I'm feeling miserable. I can't stop myself. It's sort of like a rainbow suddenly appearing smack bang in the middle of a thunderstorm. Except that it's in my head. When the rainbow appears, we both sit back and have a good chuckle because Blake says that laughter is a helpful reaction which leads to a positive feeling. But then, when we've finished having our chuckle, he says, 'Seriously though, Lottie, do you get my point?' and almost always I nod my head and say, 'Yeah I do, Blake,' because underneath all that space-age rubbish, Blake says stuff which makes total perfect sense. He is very helpful and nice and I like him. Also, he looks a lot like Johnny Depp but without the pirate make-up.

Blake is helping me to sort my head out. Usually, my head is a pretty neat place filled up with pop music and poetry and moments of total and utter Laugh Out Loud magic that I share with my BEST EVER friend, Goose. Moments like the other day when me and Goose went shopping in town and pretended for the ENTIRE TIME that we were called Janice and Jonice and that we were on a two-week vacation from Kentucky, USA. How I didn't collapse with laughter-induced breathing difficulties when Goose strolled into Gladbagz and asked to see their latest selection of fanny packs,[1] I will never know. Or like last week when we tested whether it's possible to eat a whole custard slice in one bite. (It's not.)

But last term, my head got all messed up.

None of that matters now though. Blake says I must focus on the present and not get hung up about the past. He's right. If I think too much about what happened – like how I fell down a mental manhole and how I got arrested and how I thought my house would fall down if I got out of bed – I get upset and want to scream. This isn't a helpful reaction and it doesn't lead to a nice feeling. So I'm going to bin all those crappy thoughts and focus instead on the

---

[1] This is what American people call bumbags. They also think that Randy is a perfectly acceptable name for a male human being. I know a lot about this subject because I'm a keen follower of *American Idol*.

cool stuff in my life.

Stuff like:

1. How me and

have officially been an item for six entire weeks and how I still fancy his

colossal manly thighs

and how he **still** doesn't seem to be bothered by the fact that I have a nose the same shape as a potato. Incidentally, Gareth Stingecombe is the best rugby player in my school. He's got green eyes and fluffy hair and a big smile and a cute wonky tooth. He floats my boat and tickles my fancy. (Not literally.)

2. How my NUMBER ONE friend in the whole world is Goose McKenzie, who just happens to be the coolest and cleverest girl in my school. Although interestingly, she only got an A grade for her GCSE English coursework folder – whereas I got an A★.

3. How my mum has said that if I continue going to my counselling sessions and also make a good start to Year 11, she'll buy me a baby rabbit.

So I'd better start stocking up on hay and carrots right now because Blake says that as long as I keep following the path of positivity, Year 11 should be a box of budgies.[2]

When I get my baby rabbit, I'm going to call it Hendrix – whether it's a boy rabbit or a girl rabbit. This is in honour of my most favourite dead person who has ever existed. The Late Great Jimi Hendrix. He was a Rock God Extraordinaire and the man with the best hair that has ever

---

[2] Apparently, this is how people from New Zealand say 'good'.

4

been witnessed by any living being on the face of this planet. If I had hair like Jimi's, I would look approximately like this and everybody at school would be sick with jealousy.

Sadly, I've got the common sort of hair which is very straight and very boring and definitely not an Afro. I have to go to a lot of trouble to make it look interesting. At the end of last term, when I went all weird and got totally cheesed off with my life, I stopped washing it and started to look a bit of a state. Doctor Edwards at the hospital told me I should keep an eye on my hair and use it as an indicator of potential future depressive episodes. She said that glossy, healthy hair is a sign of a happy, healthy person. This means that I'm currently as chirpy as a chipmunk because my hair, at this precise moment in time, is nothing short of SENSATIONAL. This morning, I stayed in the bath for absolutely ages and gave myself a double application of Melody Total Black-Out hair colorant so that I can start Year 11 without the shame of having any of my beige roots showing.

I am EXTREMELY impressed with the results. Something about Melody Total Black-Out has made my hair look very sleek and stylish. I actually think I quite closely resemble an Ancient Egyptian – which is an ultra-sophisticated look and a radical departure from my norm because I'm very much a modern-day kind of person and from Cardiff.[3] My new style direction has given me a pale and interesting appearance – a bit like this.

When my mum saw my new hair she said, 'Oh Lottie, you're not turning into one of those sulky gothic people, are you?'

She means goths. There are quite a lot of them in Whitchurch village where I live. When they're not in their sixth-form lessons, they sit on the bench on the traffic island in the middle of the road and look depressed.

'No,' I said. 'Of course not. Don't be daft!'

---

[3] Cardiff is the capital of Wales – whereas the capital of Egypt happens to be Cairo. I suppose, on paper, they look fairly similar.

My mum raised her eyebrows and said, 'It's *my* house. I can be daft in it whenever I like.'

'Whoops!' I said, and then, 'Sorry.' Sometimes my mouth just runs away from me and I forget who I'm talking to.

'So what's with the jet black hair then?'

'I'm rocking a new style for Year 11 because I don't want to turn up on the first day with minging beige roots. I think I look like an Ancient Egyptian.'

My mum seemed a bit surprised and then she said, 'Sorry, Cleopatra, I didn't realize. But now you've pointed it out, I can completely see that it's a very Egyptian look you're rocking.' And then she told me to go and scrub all of the black stains out of the bath.

My mum likes to think she's funny. Sometimes she is but mostly she's just toe-curlingly embarrassing. A premium example of this is when Gareth Stingecombe came round my house for the very first time. He brought the DVD of *Dumb and Dumber* with him and a massive box of rum-flavoured chocolates so that we could have a laugh and get drunk. My mum was actually very thoughtful and respected our privacy and went out for a meal with her friend. But before she went, she cornered me in the kitchen and whispered, 'I'll be home by eleven at the latest. Make sure Gareth is gone by then, and can you also make sure that he keeps it well and truly tucked inside his trousers.'

My mum is a police sergeant. You'd think that she would know better than to make criminally tasteless remarks of this nature.

As it happens, she needn't have worried. Neither Gareth nor I have done *it* yet and we aren't in any hurry to either. I've discussed our relationship with him and I've decided that we should both save ourselves until we're at least twenty-one. This will allow us the time to really get to know each other on an intellectual and spiritual level and also, by then, we'll be so desperate to do *it* that it's bound to be a more passionate and thrilling experience. Until then, I'm perfectly content with a bit of fully-clothed contact and some extended pashy snogging.

I'm going to do a swift topic shift now because this subject is making me feel a bit funny.

Blake reckons that I should try not to worry too much about what happened last term. He says that the world is a mixed-up, confusing place and I just got a bit lost for a while and it gave me an attack of the collywobbles. I've been seeing Blake every other Friday afternoon for a few weeks now and I don't mind admitting that I was very nervous to begin with. After all, he's a counsellor in an adolescent mental health unit and I'm an adolescent with a reasonably significant mental disorder. It's not a fantastic social situation to be in.

My mum came in with me the first time because I'd probably have run away otherwise. We were both quite surprised when we saw Blake because he was definitely not what we were expecting. He was young and smiley and had longish hair and was wearing flip-flops even though the rest of his clothes were quite smart. To be honest, I'd prepared myself for someone who looked a bit more like this:

And he was a man. I definitely wasn't expecting that. Especially one who looked like Johnny Depp.

Having my mum there with me made it a total waste of time. I was too embarrassed to say anything much in front of her, so instead I just sat and looked at the floor and answered everything Blake said in a mumble-grumble voice. And then, finally, his alarm clock went off. Blake always has an alarm clock in his room so that we both know exactly how much time is left in the session.

The next time I went, I made Mum wait in the reception area. Blake asked me to write a list of all the stuff I'm good at. At first, I couldn't come up with a single thing and then Blake said, 'There's no need to be cool about it. *Everyone* is good at something. I'm really good at swimming and making smoothies. Be loud and proud and write down two or three things that you can do better than most other people.' And I sat there in silence for a bit and then, because I was aware that the alarm clock would go off soon and I was running out of time, I wrote:

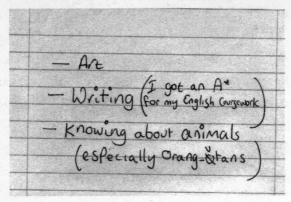

— Art
— Writing (I got an A* for my English Coursework)
— Knowing about animals (especially Orang-utans)

Blake looked at my list and said, 'Cool! You know what, Lottie, a healing mind is an occupied mind. There's something I want you to do. You're obviously good at writing. I mean – Crikey Dick![4] - you got an A★. So I want you to keep a journal—'

'I don't do diaries,' I said really quickly. This is true. I just don't see the point of them.

'Woah there!' said Blake, even quicker. 'Not a diary. A diary is a bit too blah, blah, blah. I'm talking more of a journal—'

'What's the difference?' I said.

'A journal,' said Blake, and he did this big dramatic pause and waggled his eyebrows like he was about to tell me the entire secret history of the cosmos, 'is a daily record of events!'

---

[4] I think this means BIG WOW! in New Zealandish. I shan't be saying it myself.

'That sounds like a diary,' I said. 'I don't do diaries. Or journals.'

Blake rubbed his chin. 'When I say journal, I don't actually mean that. Forget the word *journal*. I want you to do something a little more specific. I want you to keep a notepad of your emotions. An *emotion notepad*. You can use it to write down all the good things and bad things and interesting things that happen to you, and that way, it'll be easier to keep a track of your ups and downs. It'll help you contemplate life. And besides, it will sharpen that artistic talent you've got.' He put his head on one side and gave me a hopeful look. He was blatantly very excited by the prospect of an Emotion Notepad. For one moment, I almost thought he was going to start clapping. 'Reckon you can do that?'

I thought about it. 'Still sounds like a diary,' I said.

'It's not a diary,' said Blake, really quickly. 'It's an—'

'Emotion Notepad. Yeah, yeah, whatever.' I turned the idea over in my mind for a moment. It didn't seem too awful. 'I'm not writing in an actual scatty notepad, though,' I added firmly. 'I'll do it on my computer, if you don't mind. And I'll do it in my own way.' Then, almost immediately, I rolled my eyes and pulled a slightly peeved face because I suddenly felt like I'd been conned into writing something which sounded suspiciously like a diary. Blake just smiled back at me all innocently and before I could even stop myself, I realized I was smiling back at him. It's extremely difficult to argue with somebody who looks like Johnny Depp.

So now I'm sitting in my bedroom, keeping my healing mind active by typing about all this stuff and, to be honest, I'm so incredibly busy that I don't actually mind too much that it's Wednesday the 5th September tomorrow and that just happens to be the first day of Year 11!

I can handle it. I'm surfing a wave on the Sea of Tranquillity. And besides that, Gareth Stingecombe will be there by the tuck shop to meet me.

a wOBBLY MOmeNt ON the waY tO sChOOL

Even though I've had my lucky knickers[5] on all day, I have to say that so far Year 11 has been a total let-down. I have upset my mum and stropped out on Goose. On the upside, I've also discovered chinchillas, possibly got myself a new job, and written a poem which expresses the depth of my passion for Gareth Stingecombe. I wrote my poem very early this morning before I was even dressed. I don't want to sound big-headed or anything but I think it's quite good. Actually, I think it's bordering on brilliant. It's a lot more spiritual and sophisticated than anything I've previously written and I think it's easily as good as the poems we are forced to analyse at school. In fact, it's probably better. Here it is.

Sonnet to Gareth Stingecombe: Oh Why Do I Wake?

Oh why do I wake with thoughts of your thighs?

Is it because I'm thrilled and excited

By their manly strength and colossal size?

Oh why do I wake feeling delighted?

Is it because of a far distant dream

Where you run towards me, hot and breathless,

Dressed in the shirt of the Welsh rugby team?

---

[5] They have a picture of Justin Timberlake on them. YES, I KNOW I'M TRAGIC. But when I'm wearing them, I feel like I'm bringing sexy back. ☺

These dreams engulf me and I am helpless.
But Gareth, my sweet, I needn't worry,
You are more than a spectre of my mind
Who floats by night and flits in a hurry.
You're definitely real and sexy and kind.
And even when afar, you're in my thoughts,
Naked, apart from your tight rugby shorts.

It took me ages to write and it's lucky that I woke up so early or I never would have got it finished before breakfast. I always try to get up early these days. Blake says that instead of lazing around in bed, I should 'rattle my dags' and find something to keep me occupied. When I asked him exactly what he meant by this, he said, 'Do the ton . . . jump the judder bar . . . speed things up a bit in the morning and get your day off to a flying start.'

I swear to God, I know he's from New Zealand, which is where hobbits come from, but sometimes it feels like Blake is talking a totally foreign language. My English teacher, Mr Wood, would have an attack of the collywobbles if he heard him.

To the untrained eye, my sonnet may appear to be an effortless outpouring of art and emotion but, believe me, it wasn't. Sonnets are actually extremely complicated and difficult things to write and I don't think I'll bother writing another. I just don't have the time. Even so, I've now got much more respect for William Shakespeare.

Unfortunately, I made the mistake of showing my poem to Goose. In general, me and Goose are very open with each other and I feel as if I can talk to her about pretty much anything. At the end of last term, when I first started breaking out in hot flushes and a pash rash every time Gareth looked in my direction, it was Goose I turned to for guidance and advice. Just like it was Goose who turned to *me* when she thought she was growing an eleventh toe. And it was *me* who convinced her that she wasn't. But even so, there are some things I know I should keep to myself. My Justin Timberlake lucky knickers are one, and my sonnet to Gareth should have been another.

I was already slightly fed up this morning because Goose arrived at my house over ten minutes late. When I opened the door, she said, 'Sorry, Lottie. The handle fell off the bathroom door while I was cleaning my teeth and my dad had to bash the door down with a chair so that I could get out.'

Goose is always late for things and she always has a dodgy, made-up excuse to explain why. Normally, I don't mind, but on this occasion I was feeling a bit edgy because I really didn't want to be late for school and me and Gareth's romantic rendezvous round the back of the tuck shop.

Then Goose said, 'What's with the black hair? Have you turned into a goth?'

This made me feel edgier still. I grabbed my bag and my dinner ticket and said, 'Of course not. This look is blatantly inspired by the fashion choices of the ultra-chic Ancient Egyptians from Cairo.'

Goose looked a bit confused for a moment and then she said, 'Oh yeah. Now you say it, I can see it. Sort of.'

I shouted goodbye to Mum and walked with Goose towards our school. We'd barely reached the end of my road before Goose said, 'I'm thinking of forming a new band. Something a bit like the Foo Fighters – except with no male members and with a more disco sound. Do you want to join?'

I looked at Goose, surprised. I was also extremely chuffed too, if I'm honest. Goose has been making music for as long as I've known her, which is almost an entire year now, and not once has she ever asked me to join in on any of her musical projects.

'Wow . . . yeah,' I said. 'But what's happened to Goose McKenzie and the Tribe of Pixies?' I asked. 'I thought you were getting loads of interest from record companies.'

Goose pulled a face. 'Well . . . yeah, we were. Definitely. But I wanted to go in a different artistic direction. And besides, I don't want to be in a band with my baby brothers any more.'

Goose's brothers are called Bill and James. They're in Year 9 and, being twins, there are two of them. Until very recently, they were cute midgets but when I saw them the other day, they'd both grown about thirty centimetres and developed croaky voices.

I said, 'I totally want to be in your band, Goose. The only potential hitch is that I can't actually play any musical instruments. And I can't sing.'

Goose said, 'No, but you can shout in an artistic and interesting way, can't you? And maybe you could write some lyrics?'

And that was when I made my mistake. I delved into my bag and took out the piece of paper which had my sonnet to Gareth Stingecombe on it. I'd been planning to show it to my English teacher, Mr Wood. I think he's the sort of person who would be impressed by its charm and subtlety. He's a bit old and he can be fairly boring sometimes, but I respect his opinion on these matters because he gave me an A★ for my English coursework.

'You're right – I reckon I *could* write song lyrics,' I said to Goose. 'I wrote this poem when I woke up this morning and it only took me three hours.'

Goose stopped walking and looked at me. '*Three hours!* What time did you get up?'

I frowned. It already seemed like such a long time ago, I couldn't actually remember.

In a voice that sounded genuinely alarmed, Goose said, 'Lottie, you're not getting ill again, are you?'

'No, of course I'm not,' I said. 'I'm surfing a wave on the Sea of Tranquillity but I can't expect to reach the shore immediately, can I?'

Goose looked at me blankly then took the piece of paper from my hand. I held my breath while she read it.

After a minute or two, she said, 'It's *really* good, Lottie. It's got a proper rhyme scheme and everything.'

This made me feel incredibly honoured and proud. Goose is an extremely gifted poet herself so she knows what she's talking about. Usually.

I said, 'Yeah, and it's got ten beats per line and plenty of pointless unanswerable questions so it's a proper sonnet exactly like what Shakespeare would have written. I'm thinking of showing it to Mr Wood.'

Goose bit her lip for a second and then said, 'Hmmm.' And then she just said nothing.

My footsteps slowed right down and I said, 'What does that mean?'

Goose looked a bit shifty and said, 'What does *what* mean?'

'*Hmmm*,' I said. 'What does *Hmmm* mean?'

Goose looked even shiftier and bit her lip again. Finally, after a colossal pause, she sighed and said, 'Well, it's just . . . I wouldn't show it to Mr Wood if I were you.' And then she added, 'And whatever you do, I *definitely* would NEVER EVER show it to Gareth Stingecombe.'

I frowned. And then really quickly and in a blatantly annoyed voice, I said, 'I wasn't actually planning to show it to him.' This is true. Even though me and Gareth have been going out for six entire weeks, I still think it's too early to expose him to my artistic talents. He might be freaked out by my cleverness and dump me. I couldn't be bothered to explain all this to Goose though, so instead I just said, 'But what's wrong with it anyway?'

Goose said, 'I'm not being funny, Lotts, but it makes you sound like a stalker.'

This annoyed me a LOT. NO WAY am I a stalker. Nor have I EVER had any stalkerish tendencies. Goose, on the other hand, once followed Neil Adam all around Freezer World. Apparently, he bought a maxi-bag of mixed vegetables and a box of eighteen fish fingers.

Before I could remind her of this, Goose said, 'Anyway, I thought you hated poetry.'

I came to a complete halt on the pavement. Goose stopped too.

'I *used* to hate poetry,' I said, 'but that was before I fully understood its power.'

Goose smirked. 'Its *power*?'

I closed my eyes and did a big dramatic pause. And then, in my best ever intellectual voice, I said, 'One day, Gail . . . one day, you will read a piece of poetry and it will speak directly to your heart and then you will be so moved with emotion that you will cherish that poem always and then, Gail, you will understand the power of poetry. Trust me.'

I opened my eyes and started walking towards school again, secretly feeling very pleased with myself. I learned these words off by heart after Mr Wood said them to me last term. I think they sound dead clever and this moment provided the perfect occasion to use them. Also, I'd used Goose's real name and I know that really winds her up.

Goose's eyes went a bit narrow. Then she handed my sonnet back to me and said, 'OK, Charlotte *Beryl* Biggs, I'll bear that in mind.'

This time *I* went red. My middle name embarrasses me. In actual fact, I'm thinking of changing it by deed poll to something a bit more contemporary. Like Beyoncé. Or perhaps Brontë. Yeah, probably Brontë. Charlotte Brontë Biggs has got quite a sophisticated tone to it, I think.

We walked the rest of the way to school in silence. I don't like having disagreements with Goose but sometimes we get on each other's nerves. I know that now and again I can be slightly annoying but it isn't always my fault. I think Goose occasionally forgets that just because she happens to have been blessed with an amazing pair of cheekbones, it doesn't necessarily mean that she's always right about everything. In fact, sometimes she is just PLAIN WRONG.

But I still don't like it when we fall out. And to be honest I was starting to regret the whole stupid conversation. I was even starting to regret that I'd actually got out of bed in the first place. And the closer we got to the school entrance, the more I just wished and wished I was by myself, under my duvet with my bedroom light switched off.

But then I remembered what Blake had taught me about being positive. And I took all my rubbish thoughts and I did this:

It made me feel a whole lot better – although I must admit that I was still having some trouble getting over the fact that Goose had called me a stalker.

When we reached the entrance to the main school building, I hesitated for a moment and then, in my best Kentucky accent, I said, 'Share a bag of fries with you at lunchtime, Janice?'

And even though Goose was still being a bit sulky, she gave me a small grin and drawled back, 'Well, hey, I guess, Jonice.'

In my normal voice I said, 'Last one to the chippy is a useless numpty.'

And Goose made a big L-shape with her hand and held it

up in front of my face and said, 'That'll be you then, loser!'

Then we separated to go in our different directions and I walked off feeling a lot less wobbly and a whole lot happier because it seemed as though me and Goose were pretty much back to being a box of budgies again.

three Is a traGIC NumBer

When I arrived at the tuck shop, Gareth Stingecombe was turning away from the front of the queue with a hot dog in each hand. As soon as he saw me, he gave a big massive grin and shouted, 'Biggsy! Over here, Sexy!' And then, almost immediately, he crinkled his face into a frown and boomed, 'What's with the black hair?'

Gareth has got a huge and beautiful smile. This is one of the things that first attracted me to him. When he smiles, it gives me a warm glow which starts in the bottom of my stomach and spreads its way right to the very furthest tips of my fingers and toes – just like a mug of steamy hot chocolate on a cold wintry day. Other aspects of him that I really like are his thighs, which are very colossal and manly and, individually, are probably as wide as my entire body. He has also got a very loud voice. I'm less keen on this.

I walked over to him, fluttered my eyelashes teasingly and said, 'Gareth, I'm not a sex object, thank you very much.'

Gareth's cheeks went a bit red and he looked down towards his hot dogs. 'I got one for you,' he said and held it out to me. I took it and looked down at it. It was wrapped in a soggy piece of kitchen roll and was covered in tomato ketchup and mustard, which had mixed together and turned a putrid pinky-orange colour.

'Ta, Gaz,' I said. 'But I'm not really that hungry.'

Gareth went even redder and I felt a bit bad for being so

ungrateful. I've noticed that Gareth is one of those people who goes red very easily. He'd be absolutely rubbish as an international con man or a Las Vegas card player because you can always tell exactly what's going on inside his head just by looking at the colour of his cheeks. Fortunately, Gareth has already decided that when he leaves school he wants to be a professional rugby player. This is an ideal career choice because everyone has a red face when they're playing rugby. He will blend in perfectly.

'It's quarter past eight in the morning,' I said, trying to explain. 'Normally, this hot dog would look very appetizing to me but I've only just had my breakfast.'

'No worries,' said Gareth. 'I can always manage a second. Coach Jenkins says I gotta keep my bulk up for the rugby field.' And then he crammed half his hot dog into his mouth, gave a couple of slow and massive chews, and then squashed in the rest of it. I passed my hot dog back to him and he went through the process all over again. I've never seen two hot dogs disappear so fast in my entire life. To be honest, if it weren't for the fact that Gareth has an incredibly sweet face and colossal rugby thighs, I might have felt a bit sick.

'Anyway, Biggsy,' said Gareth moments later, after wiping his mouth on the sleeve of his sweatshirt. 'What's with the black hair, like? You're not going all weird and goth on me, are you?'

I gave him a moody, sexy stare. To tell the truth, I was starting to get a bit fed up with having to explain to everybody my Ancient Egyptian styling decision. So instead I just said, 'So what if I am?'

Gareth turned purple-red and said, 'Well . . . nothing really, I suppose. It's totally up to you, isn't it? And I'll always like you whatever. It's just that . . . well . . . I'd be a bit gutted if you started looking like a zombie and began shoving bolts into your face and stuff because I kind of think you actually look really incredibly pretty as you are.'

Then he smiled at me.

And a weird thing happened.

INSTANTANEOUSLY, I stopped being annoyed and started feeling actually quite stunned and amazed because this is just **not** the sort of thing that anyone who has a nose shaped like a potato expects to hear.

I smiled back at him and said, '*Incredibly* pretty?'

And Gareth turned totally scarlet-pimpernel-red and looked a bit shifty and said, 'Well, not incredibly pretty. More like *a bit* pretty. From a distance. In the dark.'

He was so embarrassed that even his ears had gone red.

I said, 'Well, for your information, I'm having a big spider's web tattooed on to my cheek this evening and I'm getting a spike put through my lip at the weekend. So deal with it, Caveman.'

And Gareth said, 'Second thoughts, Biggsy, I reckon that'd be a big improvement.'

And then he smiled another one of his massive smiles and punched me in the arm. Not hard. Just friendly. And I got that warm glow in the bottom of my stomach which spread its way right to the very furthest tips of my fingers and toes. And then I punched him back and we walked off to registration with our arms around each other.

The rest of the morning passed me by in a bit of a blur. I've always found the first day of term particularly stressful. Over the holidays you sort of forget about school, and when you have to go back it's a nasty shock. It's not easy being forced out of the house at eight in the morning to sit around all day in a place where people waffle on about random topics like William Shakespeare and Bunsen burners and Central Business Districts[6] for hours and hours on end. It isn't easy at all. In fact, I've been doing it for eleven years now and I'm still not entirely comfortable with it. To make matters even worse, Lee Fogel – who is definitely the most annoying person in my school and probably the most annoying person on the entire planet – turned up to registration with a string of putrid love bites all around his neck. I was really glad then that I hadn't eaten the hot dog that Gareth offered me because if I had done, there is a serious likelihood that I would have totally and utterly and physically hurled right then and there in the classroom.

This is the kind of horrific experience that school exposes us to on a daily basis.

I was really glad when registration was over and I could get out of that room and head off to English. Along with art and history, English is one of my all-time favourite subjects.

---

[6] This has got something to do with geography. Don't ask me what, though.

I'm genuinely quite interested in reading and writing and, also, it's one of the few lessons where I get to sit next to Goose. It's a scientifically proven fact that teenagers always work harder and get better results when they are allowed to sit next to their best friends. Anyone with half a head knows that this is absolutely true.

Mr Wood has given us a new book to read. He told us as soon as we came in that it was called *The Picture of Doreen Gray* and it was written by a very famous Irish writer called Oscar Wilde who everyone has heard of. Apparently. We spent the entire lesson just talking about Chapter One. As I said before, I'm genuinely quite interested in reading and stuff but this might be about to change. During the lesson, I got so bored I went into a trance and almost stopped breathing. I can tell you right now, Oscar's book is going to be terrifically-horrifically tedious. This is blatantly apparent just from reading the first sentence – which is this:

> *The studio was filled with the rich odour of roses, and when the light summer wind stirred amidst the trees of the garden there came through the open door the heavy scent of the lilac, or the more delicate perfume of the pink-flowering thorn.*

Mr Wood thinks it's a marvellous opening sentence. He thinks it's bursting deliciously with olfactory images. Apparently, this means we can smell it. What Mr Wood is forgetting, though, is that it's a bit hard to appreciate the *delicate perfume of the pink-flowering thorn* when:

a) You've never smelt the pink-flowering thorn and
b) You're sitting in a classroom being suffocated by olfactory images of Lee Fogel's stinky trainers and a general heavy scent of BO.

Mr Wood was walking around the classroom reading to us. It's not really his fault, I suppose, but everything he says sounds like it's coming at you through a megaphone. It's all one volume and that volume gives you a headache. As soon as he had read as far as the first full stop, he came to a standstill in front of the desk that I share with Goose, and put down his book.

'Charlotte Biggs, can you make sure you are reading along?'

'Is it OK if I just listen, Mr Wood?' I said.

Mr Wood said, 'I'd prefer it if you followed the words on the page.'

I did a big noisy sigh and sat up. I was about to open my book when I hesitated and said, 'Can I ask a question?'

Mr Wood looked at me a little suspiciously and then he said, 'Fire away, Charlotte.'

'I'm not being funny,' I said, 'but why do we have to read books about gardening anyway?'

'Gardening?'

'Yeah,' I said. 'Books which bang on about roses and lilacs and women called Doreen don't really interest me that much, to be honest.' I was being as polite and as tactful as I could. Not like Lee Fogel, who seized the opportunity to shout out, 'Yeah, sir, this book is a steaming crock of horse—'

'Thank you, Lee,' said Mr Wood very quickly. Then he smiled at me and scratched his head. 'What about if I promise you that this novel is neither about a woman called Doreen *nor* gardening. In fact, you'll see that *Dorian* Gray is a very interesting and complex *male* character. Will you give it a chance?'

I shrugged my shoulders.

Mr Wood smiled again. 'Trust me, Charlotte, I think you'll enjoy this story,' he went on, and then he said, 'Would *you* like to read to us?'

'I doubt it,' I said. But I quickly picked up my book and started reading it out loud anyway because I thought it would be a charitable act of kindness to save everyone from Mr Wood's mega-boring megaphone voice.

I'd barely been reading for a minute before Mr Wood said, 'Stop!'

And then he said,

QUIETER AND PUT MORE EXPRESSION INTO YOUR VOICE

I put my book down and looked at him to see if he was joking. He wasn't. Sometimes, I feel like I'm the only sane person in the entire world – which is weird really because I'm the only person I know who actually isn't. I'm OK most days though.

After that, I had geography.

By lunchtime, I was feeling pretty much like this:

Central Business Districts blah...blah...blah

The nanosecond that I was let out at twelve o'clock, I hurried to Pat's Plaice, the chip shop on Merthyr Road, so that I could get a good place in the queue and get myself served before the chips dried out and went too chewy. Despite our *last one's a numpty* challenge, I knew that Goose would probably be late. After all, she'd just had music and Goose is always late out of her music lessons. She is a very musically gifted person but she has a personality clash with her teacher and this means that she usually has to stay behind for a few minutes to be moaned at and issued with a detention notice.

I was next in line to be served when Goose finally arrived, all breathless from having run up the high street. She pushed her way through the queue of waiting people, handed me some change and said, 'Sorry, Lotts, I got kept behind because Mr Howells caught me playing the guitar with my teeth. Can you get me a battered sausage and chips?'

Behind us, someone started moaning about Goose pushing in. I turned round and saw that it was only Lee Fogel so I said, 'All right, don't get your pants in a pickle.' And then I got our chips and went with Goose to eat them on the pavement outside.

As we were passing through the door, Goose said, 'I hope you don't mind, Lottie, but I've invited someone else to come and eat her dinner with us.' And then she nodded her head towards the concrete ledge which ran along the front wall of the chip shop and where all the kids from my school usually sit to eat their chips.

I looked over, and a girl who was sitting on the ledge and holding a sausage roll stared back at me.

I froze.

Goose said, 'This is Sam. She's just been moved into my music class and she's brilliant. She's going to join my new band.'

And even though I kept my face under total control so that it was the perfect picture of calm, the inside of my head was an absolutely different picture. In my mind's eye, I could see my own head spinning round and round like a poltergeist and my eyes popping out of their sockets while I screamed:

'NOoo'

at the very top of my voice.

Samantha Morgan sat there with the hand that was holding her sausage roll hovering in mid-air in front of her. And then she shrugged and took a great big greedy bite.

Goose said, 'Do you two already know each other?'

I slowly ate a chip and considered how I should answer this question. I could tell her that this was Samantha Morgan . . .

Samantha Morgan!!!

. . . the very same Samantha Morgan who USED to be my friend long before Goose came to my school but who HASN'T BEEN my friend since Year 9 because she once DELIBERATELY got me into serious trouble by provoking me so much during a Welsh lesson that I accidentally smashed a window, which resulted in my temporary exclusion from school and Samantha Morgan being told by her mum to NEVER SPEAK TO ME AGAIN.

Samantha Morgan took another bite of her sausage roll and said, 'All right, Lottie?'

I gave her a nervy fake smile and ate another chip. Then I said to Goose, 'I thought I was joining your band.'

Goose looked surprised. 'Well, yeah, but you said you can't play any instruments or sing or –'

'Yeah, but I can shout in an artistic and interesting way,' I said, really quickly. 'And anyway, I was going to write some lyrics, wasn't I?'

Goose blew on the steamy end of her sausage and said, 'Well, you still can. What's the problem?'

I couldn't think of a really good response so I gave a really pathetic one instead. 'I thought it was just going to be us!'

Samantha Morgan said, 'Oh, if Lottie's gonna freak out and cause a big scene, I'm going.' And then she stood up and started brushing pastry crumbs off her school trousers.

Goose said, 'No, hang on. I want you in my band. You're really good at playing keyboards.' And then she turned to me and said, 'Think about it, Lottie. If we're going to launch a disco-based female equivalent to the Foo Fighters, we need another member. All the best bands are trios. The Sugababes are a trio. Destiny's Child were a trio. Even The Jimi Hendrix Experience were three people, weren't they?'

I knew that Goose was just trying to get around me by bringing up The Jimi Hendrix Experience, my favourite band in the entire world – even though they don't make records any more.[7]

I swallowed hard and tried to keep my voice steady. Being in Goose's band seemed like the golden opportunity of a lifetime – but it was also losing its appeal extremely fast. I desperately wanted to tell her about Samantha Morgan and the broken window and my temporary exclusion from school, but I couldn't because Samantha Morgan was just standing there with her arms crossed, giving me evils.

Goose said, 'Three is a magic number, Lottie.'

I said, 'Yeah, maybe. But, the thing is, I don't actually want to be in this band if—'

Before I could finish, Goose snapped, 'Well, fine! Don't be then.'

So I said, 'Good. Then I won't.'

And Goose said, 'Well, don't.'

And I said, 'Yeah, well, I'm not.'

And then Lee Fogel – who is officially the most annoying person in the entire history of the universe – suddenly appeared out of the chip shop and started feeding chips to

---

[7] Unfortunately, this is no longer a possibility because, as I mentioned earlier, Jimi is sadly no longer existing in our earthly mortal dimension. ☹

Samantha Morgan in a very unnecessary and frankly sick-making manner, and I realized then that it was *her* who must have given him all those hideous yucky hickeys on his neck.

I looked at Goose and said, 'It's getting a bit crowded around here. If you don't mind, I'll leave you with your new friends.'

Goose said, 'Lottie, wait . . .'

But I was already walking off towards town. I'd had enough of school for one day.

ChiNChiLLas

A chinchilla is a little fat furry thing with chicken feet and a pointy nose. It has little round ears on either side of its head and big long whiskers which stick straight out like a hairy biker's moustache. It's about the same size as a small rabbit and it is quite possibly the cutest living creature I've ever clapped eyes on. If Lee Fogel and Samantha Morgan hadn't engaged in that dodgy display of public affection outside Pat's Plaice and forced me to move to somewhere less revolting, I might have lived my whole life unaware of the existence of these fascinating little animals. But now I am aware and soon I'm going to have one all of my own. So actually, the dodgy snoggers did me a favour. I suppose this is a very good example of positive thinking.

Blake, my counsellor, reckons that physical exercise is good for the mind. He reckons that it's a scientifically proven fact. He never said those exact words, of course, but I knew what he meant. What he *actually* said was, 'It's as good as gold that working up a sweat when you're feeling glum can stop you packing a wobbly and make you feel a lot more hunky-dory. Keep yourself nice and active, Lottie – it's good for you.'

And it was this advice which was bouncing about my brain as I marched very actively away from the chip shop.

As I marched, I tried to bin all my bad thoughts but there were just too many of them. The inside of my head was starting to feel like this:

I was quite literally in a rubbish mood.

So I stopped thinking altogether and just kept marching, and pretty soon I stopped feeling bad and angry and disgusted and started feeling nothing at all. And that felt better.

And then I stopped marching and slowed down to a regular walk.

I walked past the parade of shops on Merthyr Road, past The Jean Genie hair salon (which is owned by my future mother-in-law, Jean Stingecombe), past the Dragon Coffee House (where me and Goose used to go for a double choco-mochaccino with extra cream and marshmallows – before she decided to be close personal friends with Samantha Morgan), past the Hippo Eater pub (where my mum sometimes takes me for a Hefty Hippo Club Sandwich), over the flyover (which is really quite high up and not strictly meant for pedestrians) and all the way into Cardiff city centre.

And when I got there, I got on a bus.

And then I did what I always do when I get on a double-decker bus. I climbed up the twisty stairwell to the top deck so I could sit at the front and pretend to be flying. But to my annoyance the front seats were already taken. A girl who looked hardly any older than me was sitting with a little tiny boy who was eating a massive great bag of crisps and on the other side, a chubby middle-aged couple were rubbing noses and kissing and giggling. It was a blatant waste of a front seat because they weren't even looking out of the window.

I tutted to myself and then I said,

'Yuck!'

Actually, I think I said it louder than I meant to because the chubby man pulled his chubby face away from his chubby girlfriend and, in a slightly raised voice, said to me, 'You're sexually frustrated, you are.' He said these words with as much certainty as he might have said, 'This is the bus to Newport, this is.' Or 'I am a chubster, I am.' And then he went right back to rubbing noses with his girlfriend.

I stared at him in total gobsmacked horror and then I turned and walked right down to the other end of the bus, as far away as possible, and sat on the long back seat.

No sooner had I sat down than an old woman in the next seat pulled the sleeve of my coat and said, 'You going anywhere nice, love?'

I turned and looked at her. She had curly white hair and was wearing a bright red woolly coat. She looked quite sweet actually. In fact, now I think about it, she looked exactly like one of Santa's little helpers.

'I doubt it,' I said, and then I smiled so that she wouldn't think I was being rude.

'Gonna meet someone special, are you?' she said.

'I doubt it,' I said and then, guessing that she might be a bit lonely and wanting to talk, I asked, 'Are you?'

Santa's little helper leaned forward and said in a hushed voice, 'Who knows?' And then, in an even lower voice, she added, 'I'll be meeting my maker soon enough but only He knows if it'll be today.'

'Oh,' I said, and immediately wished I'd never asked.

She pulled the sleeve of my coat again and said, 'Day off from school, is it?'

I wasn't sure how to answer this question so I said, 'Hmmm.'

The old woman said, 'What's *Hmmm* supposed to mean?' and then, before I could even answer, she gave a big crackly laugh and said, 'You're on the mitch, ain't you? I can tell. I sees it all the time on these buses.'

I was a bit annoyed then. I said, 'It's not illegal for me to ride on a bus, you know.'

The old woman stopped laughing and said, 'Oooh, touchy! I've hit a nerve, haven't I, love? You *is* on the mitch, ain't you!'

'No, actually,' I said. 'I don't go to school any more. I left ages ago.' I didn't mean to lie but she forced me to.

'And how old would you be now then?' asked the old lady – who I'd begun to realize was not as sweet as she looked.

'Twenty-three,' I muttered. Even as I was saying it, I knew it was stupid.

'Twenty-three?' The old woman started laughing so hard that, for a moment, I thought her teeth were going to fall out. 'Twenty-three,' she said. 'Well, let me tell you something, love: today you might be twenty-three but you'll wake up tomorrow and you'll be twenty-five. The day after that, you'll wake up and be celebrating your fortieth. Before you know it, you're drawing your pension and by the end of the week, you're breathing your last breath and dropping down dead. Mark my words, kiddo, that's how fast life goes. So don't wish it away.' And then she clicked her fingers to show me how quickly my life was going to disappear.

I stood up and pressed the bell and muttered, 'Excuse me, I have to get off now.' And then I hurried down to the front of the bus – taking care not to attract the attention of the chubby man – and almost fell down the twisty stairwell in my desperation to escape.

I think it'll be a while before I get back on a Cardiff bus.

The bus pulled away, leaving me next to a small retail park. There was nothing much there except a shop called Happy Pets, a carpet warehouse and a kitchen showroom. Automatically, I started walking towards the pet store. For a crazy second I actually managed to convince myself that I *was* twenty-three and I was on my way to work on the checkouts in the pet store, but then the moment passed and I remembered that I was actually only fifteen and was mitching off school and had just been told by a random fat man on a bus that I was sexually frustrated. This didn't help improve my mood. I don't mind admitting that by the time I crossed the massive car park and walked through the doors of the pet store, I was feeling fairly miserable.

And that's when I saw it. It was sitting in a cage, all cuddled up in a corner, and it looked a bit like this:

only cuter.

I stood and looked at it for about half an hour and then a sales assistant came and asked me if I needed any help and I said, 'It's OK, I'm getting help from a behaviour therapy counsellor, but thanks anyway.'

The sales assistant gave me a weird look and walked off.

The little fat chinchilla thing yawned, closed its eyes and went to sleep. And I smiled, said bye to it, and left the shop so I could begin my very long walk home.

hOw MItChING Off sChOOL MaDe MY Mum GO eDGY aND hOw Gareth stINGeCOmBe MaDe everYthING Ok aGaIN

And then my mum stressed out on me. She must have been hovering around just waiting to pounce the very second I got home because as soon as I put my key in the lock, she flung open the door and said, 'Where on earth have you been?'

I said, 'Shouldn't you be at work?'

My mum said, 'And shouldn't you have been at school?' And then she gave me a Stare of Death and made me feel bad.

I stomped into the kitchen, threw my bag on the floor and sat down at the table with my chin in my hands. And then, because I was feeling a bit bleak and couldn't really cope with being polite, I said, 'I asked first.'

'No you didn't, *I* did,' snapped my mum. Then she sat down opposite me. 'The school phoned me at work to say that you weren't in your art lesson. I knew something must have gone wrong because you love art. I've been sitting here, worried sick, all afternoon. Now will you please tell me where you've been?'

I rolled my eyes to the ceiling and pulled my best harassed face. Then I did this:[8]

---

[8] I know it's not really for me to say – but in real life I am better looking than this picture suggests.

'Don't do that *Talk to the hand* thing to me – it's rude,' said my mum. 'Now please will you tell me what happened?'

'I didn't have a good day,' I said. 'Blake says that if I feel myself going edgy, I should bush out for a while.'

'*What?*' My mum looked confused.

I sighed again. 'What he means is – if I feel things are going wrong, I should try to remove myself to a more calming environment.' Then I added, 'Remember – Blake is from New Zealand. He speaks foreign but he makes perfect sense to me. And he's good looking.'

My mum said, 'Yes he is, isn't he? He's very good looking.' And then she went quiet and her head seemed to drift off into outer space.

'All right,' I said, suddenly feeling a bit freaked out. 'There's no need to go on about it. There are more important things in life than good looks, you know.'

My mum's head smacked back down from outer space with a thud and she said, 'Yes . . . well . . . I don't think he meant that you should truant from school and worry everyone half to death though.'

'I wasn't mitching,' I said. 'Not really. Not when you properly think about it.' And then I stopped because I knew that, actually, I'd been quite blatantly mitching and this line of argument wasn't really going to get me anywhere. I changed tack. 'Sorry.'

My mum frowned and then she sort of smiled and reached across the table and took hold of my hand. 'Promise me you won't go walking out of school again.'

My cheeks went a bit hot and my eyes started prickling. I could feel that I was dangerously close to crying. I said, 'I promise I'll *try* but it's a bit hard when your so-called best friend decides she's going to be number-one-chums with Samantha flipping Morgan.'

My mum said, 'Ah . . . I see.'

Of course, she knows about my history with Samantha. And how I got excluded in Year 9 because I threw Samantha's stupid exercise book and bag out of the window during a Welsh lesson.[9] But I only did it because she said my mum was a rozzer and I thought she'd said lezzer. Looking

---

[9] I would have thrown her chair out too but I couldn't make it fit through the gap.

back on it now, I can't believe I got so freaked out. Anyone would think I had some serious issues.

Mum said, 'Just because Goose has found a new friend, doesn't mean that she isn't still best friends with you. They say three is a magic number, you know.'

'Oh, don't start that,' I said.

'I'm just asking you to give school a chance.' My mum shrugged. 'And remember, we were going to go to the pet shop and choose a baby rabbit, weren't we?'

I sniffed and nodded. Then I said, 'Mum, instead of a rabbit, do you think I could have a chinchilla?'

My mum looked surprised. 'A chinchilla? Are they those round fluffy things with pointy faces?'

I nodded. 'Yeah. And they've got chicken feet and they sleep a lot. Can I have one?'

'I suppose so,' my mum said.

And then I felt quite happy and gave her a kiss on the cheek and was about to go upstairs when she stopped me in my tracks.

'Oh, and Lottie . . .' she called, 'Gareth popped round on his way home. He wondered if you'd be interested in a Saturday job at his mum's hair salon. There's a vacancy, apparently. If you fancy it, he said you should stop by for an interview after school tomorrow.'

I came back into the kitchen; my mouth open in amazement. 'Are you both nuts?' I said. 'I got sacked from my last job for nicking shoes during my mental-disturbance-of-a-reasonably-significant-nature episode,[10] remember?'

My mum said, 'Hmmph.' And then she said, 'Yes, I do remember that, thank you.' She raised her eyebrows and added, 'But I suppose there's nothing much to pinch in Jean Stingecombe's hair salon, is there? A few grey curls, maybe? Some split ends?'

I bit my lip. To be honest, I've always quite fancied the idea of working in a salon. I'm naturally and genuinely very interested in hair. Much more than I am in Central Business Districts or Oscar Wilde's books about gardening. I wasn't sure about working for Gareth's mum though, cos I don't know her. And although it doesn't always seem like it, I'm actually quite shy. I said, 'Does Gareth's mum know that I am an ex-criminal with a mental disturbance of a reasonably significant nature?'

My mum said, 'Stop exaggerating, please. You're not a criminal, Lottie. You don't even have a record. You were given a warning.' Then she walked over to me and put her hands on my cheeks. 'Besides, you're fine. Remember what Doctor Edwards has been telling you – and Blake too. Lots of people go through episodes of rocky mental health. It's just important that you develop strategies to cope with it.'

'But—'

'Gareth's mum wants someone like you to help out with a few odd jobs in the salon on a Saturday. And Gareth

---

[10] This is officially what is wrong with me. Doctor Edwards who works at the hospital said so. Sometimes I think it would be easier to tell people I had fleas. Or flatulence.

obviously trusts you to do a good job. And so do I.'

And then she gave me a kiss right in the middle of my forehead and I said, 'Urrgghhh, Mum, get off me, you weirdo!' But actually I was feeling very happy indeed and I ran up the stairs two at a time so that I could switch on my computer and write it all up in my Emotion Notepad Document. And that's what I've been doing pretty much ever since. But now I'm going to bed because it's already twenty past one tomorrow morning and I'm as sleepy as a chinchilla.

the JeaN GeNIe

I am a very interesting and complex character. I am a daughter, a sister, a girlfriend, a schoolgirl, a writer, a teenager, an artist, a friend, a poet, a Welsh person, a patient, a pain, a nutcase, a potato face, an animal lover, a laugh, an Egyptian trendsetter, a freethinker AND an individual.

I am also getting increasingly fed up with the continuing disloyal behaviour of my so-called best friend Goose, but I'll bin that thought for the moment and concentrate instead on a much more positive and exciting piece of news.

And that positive and exciting piece of news is this: in addition to all the above, I am now a proud employee of the Jean Genie hairdressing establishment. I even have my own official badge.

Jean Stingecombe, my new manageress and future mother-in-law, made it for me using a little plastic machine which looked like it was probably invented by a Victorian. It's not the most brilliant badge I've ever seen but, to be honest, I don't care. I've never been given a name badge before and I think my job title sounds fairly sophisticated.

Until today, I'd never actually met Gareth's mum. So far, Gareth has always come over to my house because he says his parents would hang around us and embarrass him if we went to his. Gareth says that they sometimes fuss around him too much because he doesn't have any brothers or sisters to distract them. Gareth says that he is a *fils unique*. He doesn't like being called an only child because it makes him sound lonely whereas *fils unique* makes him sound exotic and special. I can't honestly agree that I think Gareth is exotic but I do think he is fairly special. Incidentally, I sometimes feel that I can understand how it must feel to be a *fils unique* because although I have a brother and a sister neither of them live at home with me. My five-year-old brother lives with my dad and his new wife, Sally, in Wrexham. Technically, he is my half-brother and he is called Caradoc. I've also got a sister called Ruthie who is away at university. She is actually twenty but she acts as if she's five.

When I went for my interview, straight after school today, I was feeling a bit stressed out and nervous. To be fair, it's not easy meeting your future mother-in-law and being cross-examined for a job all at the same time. I was really concerned in case she thought I was a loser. But Jean Stingecombe is very nice. For an older person, she still has a reasonably pretty face and she wears her scissors in a leather holster around her waist which makes her look quite cool. I'm not at all surprised that she is nice because she is Gareth's mum and Gareth is EXTREMELY nice and has very muscular and colossal thighs. As far as I can tell,

Jean's thighs look quite tiny, but, then again, it's hard to judge because when I saw her she was wearing culottes. I've always been aware of the existence of culottes because occasionally I get dragged out shopping with my mum and she forces me to wait around like a lemon while she tries on EVERY SINGLE ITEM in a shop called Vogue Marché. Despite dropping French at the end of Year 9, I happen to speak enough of it to know that Vogue Marché means *Fashion Market*.[11] Vogue Marché is jam-packed with culottes and cords and batwing jumpers and many other blatantly dodgy clothing articles. Even so, I've never seen anyone actually wearing culottes in public. I have to admit that they did detract from Jean's coolness a little bit. Maybe when me and Jean know each other a bit better, I'll say something to her.

Despite the culottes, Jean Stingecombe is a very friendly and professional person and she runs a tight ship at The Jean Genie hairdressing salon. After we'd said hello to each other, she said, 'I run a tight ship here, Lottie. I might not be Vidal Sassoon or Nicky Clarke but them names don't mean nothing to my customers. In this patch of Cardiff, it's my name that people trust. I've got the responsibility of running the top hair salon in the whole of Whitchurch village. People come in here looking tired and dowdy and they walk out of my door feeling like minor royalty. It's a wonderful way to earn a living but it's also a lot of pressure. To cope with that

---

[11] Which is quite odd really because *Vogue Marché* is neither fashionable nor actually a market.

pressure, I need the support of an exceptional team. People I can rely on. People with a passion for customer care. People with a sense of shared responsibility. Do you have what it takes to be a part of my team, Lottie?'

I nodded and said yes. I didn't even have to think about it. For starters, I really need the extra cash because hair dye does not come cheap and, for seconds, I'm not that freaked out by the responsibility of working at Whitchurch's top hair salon. It's the only one there is. And it's a little bit cluttered and scruffy, to tell the truth. And it smells of perm solution.

Jean Stingecombe said, 'Good answer.' Then she said, 'And how do you feel about talking to members of the general public? You'll have a lot of face-to-face contact as well as telephone communication to deal with.'

I hesitated and then I said, 'I'll smile and be polite.' And then I hesitated again, before adding, 'Unless I'm on the phone – in which case, I'll just be polite.'

Jean said, 'You should still smile even if you're talking on the phone. A smile is a multi-sensual thing. It's not just visual. You can feel a smile and you can hear it too, my lovely. Didn't you know that?'

I went a bit red and tried to think of something good to say. Fortunately, the wise words of Mr Wood popped into my head. 'It's not olfactory, though,' I said. 'You can't smell a smile.'

Jean looked a bit surprised and then she said, 'Er . . . no. You can't. There's some truth in that.'

I felt quite pleased. I'd be prepared to bet all the money in the world that Jean Stingecombe didn't actually know what 'olfactory' meant.

'And how about punctuality, Lottie?' said Jean, once she'd recovered from the shock of my gargantuan vocabulary. 'Can I rely on you to arrive at my salon on time?'

I thought about this for a second and then I said, 'In my opinion, to be early is to be on time, to be on time is to be late and to be late is unacceptable.'

This is something I once got told when I was working as a Saturday Sales Assistant in a shoe shop. I think it's possibly the most tragic thing that anyone has ever said to me in my whole life. It's worth remembering though.

Jean Stingecombe looked impressed and nodded enthusiastically. 'That's a *wonderful* answer, Lottie. Now just one final question – and it's a very important one. What are you like at making tea?'

I smiled a big multi-sensual smile and said, 'Brilliant. My mum says I probably make the best cup of tea in the whole of Wales.'

This is true. I make perfect tea. Not too strong. Not too weak. Next time I see Blake, I will tell him that I've remembered something else that I'm good at.

In comparison, my older sister Ruthie is a completely rubbish tea maker. Fortunately, she is mostly in Aberystwyth so we don't have to drink her manky tea very often.

Jean Stingecombe gave me a big multi-sensual smile back and said, 'Well, Lottie, the job's yours, my lovely. You can start this Saturday.' And then she touched my arm and said, 'I'm really looking forward to working with you. I've heard so much about you from my Gazzy. He's pleased as punch about you, love. He's never had a girlfriend before.'

I went redder than a rugby player and wondered what kind of stuff Gareth had been saying about me to his mum. I really hope he never told her what I said about getting a spike put through my lip because it wasn't actually true anyway and I wouldn't want her to get the wrong idea about me. I really hope he never told her about my mental problems either.

While I was thinking all this, Jean patted my arm again and said, 'Before you go, I'd just like to introduce you to Dilys. As Junior Stylist, Dilys is a very important member of the crew. I'm the salon's Senior Stylist and the other team member is Neil. He only started with us a couple of weeks ago and he's our Trainee Stylist. Unfortunately, I can't introduce you to him now because it's his day at college.'

She opened a small door at the back of the salon and called upward, 'Dil . . . I know it's your tea break, love, but come and say hello to Lottie. She's going to be our new Salon Assistant!'

I stood there awkwardly and listened as the sound of footsteps clomped about above my head. Jean Stingecombe picked up a broom and began to sweep random silver curls into a corner and as she did, she wiggled her bottom and sang something like, '*Yoo-hoo make me feeeeel, yoo-hoo make me feeeeel, yoo-hoo make me feeeeeeeel like an act-u-al wo-man,*' along to a putrid soppy love song which was coming from a small speaker mounted on the wall. I chewed my fingernails and felt a bit embarrassed and wished Dilys would hurry up. A moment later, a face popped through the doorway and said, 'Oooh! So you're Gazzy's girlfriend! Jean's been telling me all about you. Lovely to have you join our team. We've got a tight little ship here – oh, I'm Dilys by the way.'

My entire face turned rhubarb-red again and I made a stupid squeaky sound that was meant to mean 'hello'.

In my defence, I was caught a little off guard. Dilys, the Junior Stylist, didn't really match my idea of what a Junior Stylist might look like. Most people I've seen who get jobs in hair salons have amazing hairstyles and wear chic black clothes and look so cutting edge that they should be hanging in the Tate Modern. Whereas Dilys was like this:

She looked more like a Senior Citizen than a Junior Stylist.

She was wearing culottes too. And a dodgy black T-shirt with silver sequins on it. She must have known what I was thinking because she winked at me and said, 'It's never too late to teach this old dog some new tricks,' and then she popped a mint humbug into her mouth and started to laugh.

I squeaked again and decided that it wasn't even worth trying to guess what Neil the Trainee Stylist would look like. Although it seemed pretty safe to assume that he'd be at least seventy.

'Is there anything I need to bring with me on Saturday?' I asked – because I've always been told that it's good to ask at least one question yourself when you have an interview.

Jean Stingecombe leaned on her broom and beamed back at me. 'Just a great big smile and a bag full of confidence.' And then she made me my funny name badge and, with a big rush of relief, I said goodbye and left.

what I saw whILe I was UPsIDe DOwN

To my surprise, Gareth was waiting for me outside the salon. He'd come straight from rugby practice and hadn't bothered to get changed out of his dirty kit. I don't mind admitting that my stomach went a bit funny when I saw him. In a good way, though. Not in a food poisoning kind of way. He was leaning against a lamp post a little further down the street and trying to balance a rugby ball on his head. When he saw me, he let the ball drop into his hands and shouted, 'Biggsy! Over here.'

I walked over to him and kissed him on the side of his face. His skin felt slightly prickly next to my lips. For some reason, this made my stomach go even funnier. In fact, my insides were hopping about so much I'm surprised that they didn't just hop right out of me and start jumping around on the pavement. I got a bit flustered then so I said, 'Gareth, do you have to call me Biggsy? It doesn't make me feel very sexy, actually.' And then I noticed that he'd got something weird stuck to the bridge of his nose and added, 'What's that thing on your face?'

Gareth looked confused. 'But yesterday you said you didn't want me to treat you like a sex object.' And then he said, 'Nasal strips. Coach Jenkins says I should try to wear them as often as possible to open up my airways. He reckons it'll help me get more oxygen to the tactical part of my brain and, thereby, enhance my overall performance on the field of play.'

'Yeah,' I said. 'But it would be nice if you'd make me feel like an actual woman once in a while.' And then I added, 'I'm not being funny, Gareth, but those nose plasters make you look slightly odd, *thereby* being a bit of a turn-off.'

Gareth went really red. 'OK, Lottie, I'll call you Lottie. Is that all right with you, Lottie?'

'That would be ideal,' I said.

'But the nasal strips are staying,' he said firmly. 'Rugby is not a pastime – it's a way of life, and I'm gonna do whatever Coach Jenkins reckons will help me get to the top. So you're just going to have to get used to it, Biggsy.'

And then he gave me a cheeky smile and winked at me in a deliberately suggestive manner.

I pretended his wink had no effect on me and did a big noisy sigh and rolled my eyes upward but secretly I was a bit pleased and ever so slightly erotically charged. I know that this probably isn't a politically correct and twenty-first-century-feminist-friendly thing to say but I quite like it when Gareth sets his mind to something and won't let me totally boss him about. There's no way I'd EVER tell him this though. So instead I just said, 'Why are you waiting out here? Why didn't you come into the salon and say hello to your mum like any *normal* son would?'

Gareth pulled a face. 'Nah. I'd rather see you out here. To be honest, I'm avoiding Dilys. Last time I went in there, she pinched my bum and told me I was a great big hunk of chunk. I can't handle that, Lottie. Not from her. So I'm keeping out of her way.'

I laughed in disbelief. 'Dilys? That sweet old lady?'

Gareth looked serious. 'I'm telling you, Lottie, she may *look* sweet but she's got a filthy mouth on her. And she's a sex maniac. You be careful working with her. She could be a bad influence.'

I laughed again. I couldn't help it. I don't mind admitting that it felt REALLY NICE to be standing out in the street with Gareth, just having a great big noisy public laugh, especially when school hasn't been all that brilliant recently. Today, I did at least manage to sit through every lesson without going on the mitch – but Mr Thomas had a moan at me for dozing off during double Science[12] and Goose still thinks that Samantha Morgan is more wondrously wonderful than Wonder Woman. So hearing that Dilys has got sexual designs on my boyfriend cheered me up no end. I said, 'Maybe working with Dirty Dilys and your mum is going to be more fun than I thought.' And then I pinched Gareth's muddy bottom and asked, 'Are you gonna walk me home then, you great big hunk of chunk?'

Gareth said, 'That's it! I've had enough of you, Lottie Biggs.' And then he lifted me right off the ground and up over his left shoulder so that I was practically upside down and my head was hanging down his back and my feet were wiggling around in mid-air and then he ran with me down the road like that and both of us were laughing and screaming our heads off.

---

[12] It wasn't my fault. He was talking about the periodic table.

Gareth is extremely strong.

He ran with me all the way down Merthyr Road. I think he thought I was a rugby ball. I was laughing so hard that I could hardly breathe and when I wasn't laughing, I was shouting, 'Gareth, put me down, you maniac!'

But actually, I didn't want him to put me down because it felt really nice having his arms wrapped tightly around my legs and it was also really interesting and funny seeing the world from an upside-down perspective. It's not a perspective I get to appreciate very often.

We went by:

and then we went by the second-hand record shop called:

and we even went by the shoe shop called:

where I used to work. And the next thing I knew, we were
passing the bus stop and we were both still laughing our
heads off and then I looked at the bus shelter and I saw this
written on it in marker pen:

And suddenly, the upside-down world stopped looking
like a funnier and more interesting place and just looked
blatantly weird.

I said, 'Gareth, put me down, will you?'

And Gareth just kept laughing and lumbering along the
street, so I said, 'GARETH, PUT ME DOWN, PLEASE!'

And Gareth must have sensed that I wasn't laughing any more because, just for once, he let me boss him about and actually did as he was told.

'What's up, Biggsy?' he said, once I was back on my feet.

I walked back to the bus shelter and looked at the graffiti written on the side and this time my eyes were the right way up. It said:

which is exactly what I'd thought it said the first time I read it. I stood there staring at it in surprise and tried to work out what it meant. It *definitely* said Goose. I only know ONE person called Goose and that person is (allegedly) my best friend. There isn't anyone else called Goose in my school. As far as I'm aware, there isn't anyone else called Goose in the whole of Cardiff. It's possible that Goose is actually the only Goose in the entire country of Wales.[13]

---

[13] It's NOT a principality – it's a PROPER country. Ask anyone who lives here.

I turned to Gareth and said, 'Have you seen this? It says Goose loves Spud.'

Gareth said, 'So?'

I said, 'So . . . ? So . . . ? So what does it mean?'

Gareth looked at me as if I were thick. 'It means that Goose loves Spud,' he said.

Spud is Gareth's friend. They play video games and listen to U2 songs together. Spud is quite good-looking. The reason why everyone calls him Spud is because his real name is Edward King which, in reverse, is the name of a famous English potato. The last I knew of anything, Spud was going out with Beca Bowen, who is in my registration group.

I said, 'How can Goose love Spud? She'd have told me.'

Gareth shrugged. 'Well, they're going out together, I can tell you that much.'

'WHAT?' I said. 'WHAT did you just say?'

Gareth said, 'I just said that they're going out together.'

I looked at him in amazement. 'They can't be,' I said. 'She'd have told me.'

The tops of Gareth's ears went a bit pink and he started to look uncomfortable. 'Goose and Spud. Spud and Goose. They're an item. Have been for at least a week. I thought everyone knew.'

'WHAT?' I said. 'How can Goose and Spud have been going out for AT LEAST A WEEK? We've only been back at school a couple of days! And anyway, SHE'D HAVE TOLD ME!'

Gareth shrugged and this time he didn't say anything.

I stared at the graffiti in confused silence for a moment and then my eyes flicked across the road to where Samantha Morgan and Lee Fogel had emerged from the doorway of the Dragon Coffee House. They were leaning against the cafe window and Lee was sucking Samantha's neck.

'YUCK!' I muttered in disgust. I must have muttered it a bit too loudly though because Gareth said, 'Oh, lighten up, Lottie. They're only kissing.'

And then he stooped down and brought his face right close up to mine and put his lips on top of my lips and I have to admit that, in this context, there is actually nothing yucky about the experience at all.

fLatteNING the humPs

This afternoon, I had another session with Blake the not-remotely-ugly counsellor from New Zealand. I'm glad I did because I had quite a lot of negative stuff that I needed to work through with him. When he saw me, he said, 'Hiya, Lottie. Howzit going?' and then he set the timer on his alarm clock and placed it on the desk next to us.

I said, 'It's going quite shittily to be honest, Blake,' and then I clenched my left hand into a fist and started chewing my knuckles because I knew I'd just sworn and I wasn't totally sure whether Blake would be hunky-dory with that.

Blake frowned. 'Hmmm. That good, eh?'

I stopped chewing my knuckles and relaxed slightly. If Blake was offended by my language, he wasn't showing it. But now I come to think of it, I've seen some of the other teenagers who visit the adolescent mental health unit where Blake's room is and most of them look a lot more messed up than me. I wouldn't be at all surprised if Blake gets to hear stuff which is more challenging than the word 'shittily.'

I said, 'Yeah, well . . . so much for being a surfer on the Sea of Tranquillity – I actually feel like I'm on a jet ski to Hell. Since I saw you last, my best friend has started acting all weird, a total stranger on a bus told me I'm sexually frustrated and then another random bus passenger told me I'm about to die.'

Blake said, 'Which of those things most gives you the hump?'

I tried thinking about it but I was too wound up to be able to concentrate properly and, to be honest, it seemed like a totally stupid question because none of these situations are what you might exactly call ideal. So I just said, 'THEY *ALL* GIVE ME THE SODDING HUMP.'

Blake sat back in his chair and stroked his chin.

After a minute or so of total silence, I said, 'Well, they *do* all give me the hump.' I didn't say it quite as nastily this time though.

Blake said, 'Maybe what you need to think about is *why* these situations have occurred. That way, you can try to avoid them happening again in the future. Did you start keeping that diary like I asked you to?'

'I don't do diaries,' I said really quickly.

'Not diary,' said Blake, even quicker. 'I meant to say *Emotion Notepad*. Have you started writing it?'

I nodded. 'So far, I've written about twelve and a half thousand words. But I only started it four days ago.'

Blake's eyes widened and, for a second, he seemed to forget what he was about to say. Then he said, 'Crikey Dick! Well, that'll certainly do for starters.'

'I've printed some off. Do you want to read it?' I asked.

Blake smiled and shook his head. 'It's private stuff. You're not writing it for me; you're writing it for yourself.'

'I'm writing it because *you* asked me to,' I reminded him.

Blake smiled again. 'Fair point. But the thing that matters is that you're keeping a record of the events which make you feel a bit up and down. And that will help you get your head around it all. So let's start with these random people on the bus. What did you say about them in your Emotion Notepad?'

I didn't need to get my printed pages out of my bag because I could still remember very clearly what I'd said.

'First of all there was a chubby fat man and he was rubbing noses with his chubby girlfriend and then they were kissing and then I said, "Yuck,"' I said.

Blake looked thoughtful for a second and then he said, 'Let's look at it from a different angle. How do you think that this chubby feller might have felt when you said yuck at the sight of him kissing his girl?'

I frowned and started to bite my thumbnail. I wasn't feeling very comfortable. In fact, I was feeling so completely uncomfortable that I was starting to wish that I was back in double science listening to Mr Thomas talk about the periodic table. If I had to put my finger on the cause of my discomfort, I'd say that I'd probably just realized that I'm not actually any good at seeing things from a different angle. Sometimes, I get so carried away with being me that I forget about how different it must be to be someone else.

Eventually, with my eyes firmly glued just to the left of Blake's head, I said, 'I probably aggravated him.'

Blake hunched his shoulders and gave me a little shrug which seemed to say that he agreed with me. 'Chances are that he'd be wanting to say something ratty right back at you. Negativity breeds negativity. And what about the other person on the bus?'

'She told me I'd be dead by the end of the week,' I said.

Blake raised his eyebrows. 'That's a strange thing to say to someone.'

I scratched my head. I was starting to feel confused. It did seem an odd comment for a random stranger to have made. 'Hold on a minute,' I said to Blake and pulled my papers out of my bag. I shuffled through them and found the bit about the bus and re-read my words from two days earlier.

When I'd finished reading, I felt a bit stupid. 'I think she was just annoyed because I'd lied to her about my age,' I mumbled.

'Well, there you go,' said Blake. 'Two easy ways to avoid getting the hump in the future. Don't tell people that the sight of them snogging makes you wanna chuck up and don't tweak the truth. Does that seem so awful?'

'I suppose not,' I said.

'Now, what about this best friend of yours?'

When Blake said this, my face fell and I realized that the words of a million stroppy strangers on a bus couldn't worry me more than the fact that me and Goose aren't talking.

I said, 'Goose is going out with Spud and everyone knows about this except me, apparently, and I'm supposed to be her best friend.'

Blake said, 'Have you asked her why she hasn't said anything?'

I shut my eyes for a second and rubbed my forehead,

which was starting to ache. 'I was going to say something this morning cos we usually walk to school together but then I remembered that she prefers to hang out with Samantha Morgan these days so I got the hump and walked to school on my own.'

Blake looked even more thoughtful and then he said, 'Who is Samantha Morgan?'

'Someone who once called my mum a rozzer – only I thought she said lezzer, and so I threw her stuff out of the classroom window and got excluded. I don't like her much.'

Blake said, 'You seem quite upset with Goose. Perhaps you just need to have a proper talk to her about these things.'

I bit my thumbnail and stared into space, somewhere just to the right of Blake's head. I was having problems looking him straight in the eye.

'If you talk to Goose, what's the very worst that could happen?' asked Blake.

'She could say something I don't like which might cause me to start chucking her things out of the window and then I'll get excluded and fail all my GCSEs and not be allowed into the sixth form and feel a total sad failure for the rest of my life,' I said.

When I said this Blake looked worried. 'OK,' he said, 'then how about you talk to her in a less direct way. Over the phone or on the Internet. What could be the worst that would happen then?'

'One of us would slam the phone down or else my paranoid mum would walk in and see I was using an Internet chat room and think I was talking to a sixty-year-old Texan man and ban me forever from the computer.'

'And the best that could happen?' asked Blake.

'Me and Goose would get talking again,' I said.

And then Blake's alarm clock went off and I knew what I needed to do.

GOOse MCkeNzie thINks she's ChOCOLate

It was gone three o'clock by the time I got back to my mum. She was sitting in her car and reading a newspaper. When she saw me, she folded up her newspaper and said, 'Session OK?'

'Not bad,' I said.

My mum gave me a shifty smile and said, 'Was Blake looking as handsome as ever?'

I glanced sharply at my mum. She'd turned a bit pink. 'I didn't particularly notice,' I muttered.

My mum giggled and turned on the ignition. Frowning so hard that it made my face hurt, I stared out of the passenger-side window and ignored her. Being the child of a criminally tasteless police sergeant gets me down sometimes.

I stared out of the window all the way home and as we got closer and closer to our house, I saw that the streets were already filling up with kids from my school. It occurred to me that I'd just LEGALLY missed an ENTIRE AFTERNOON of double science and, instantly, this made me smile. But only for one micro-second. Because then, I thought about Goose and how I needed to have a serious conversation with her about some serious matters and I stopped smiling and just felt anxious.

Once we were back inside the house, my mum put her arm across my shoulders and said, 'How about a quick game of Sonic the Hedgehog with me before I start tea?'

I shrugged my shoulders and said, 'Nah, it's boring – you always beat me.' And then I said, 'Besides, I need to go upstairs and have a private telephone conversation with Goose.'

My mum looked puzzled. 'Can't you just catch her as she walks by from school and save yourself some credit?'

I said, 'It's complicated. I've got things I need to get off my chest and Blake recommends that I speak to her in a less direct manner.'

My mum shot me a suspicious glance. Then she said, 'Well, don't give Goose a hard time. Friends like her can't be ordered out of a catalogue.'

'What's that supposed to mean?' I said.

'Exactly what you think it means,' said my mum. 'Goose is a good friend to you and you haven't always been the easiest person to get along with.'

For a moment, I just stood and stared at her in total disbelief. And then I said, 'Why are you having a go at me?'

My mum opened her mouth and then she closed it again and just sighed. Finally, after a long pause, she said, 'I'm *not* having a go at you, Lottie. I'm really proud of how well you've been coping recently. You've got a gorgeous boyfriend, you're back at school, you're really positive about these counselling sessions with Blake and you're about to start a new Saturday job. You're brilliant! Just remember, please, that Goose is very much a part of your recovery.'

I went red and smiled. 'Gareth is gorgeous though, isn't he?'

'He's good enough to eat,' said my mum and kissed me on the nose. 'And so is Goose.'

'Yeah, whatever,' I said and rubbed the kiss off. Quite blatantly, my mum thinks Goose should get a *Heart of Gold* award just for putting up with me.

Upstairs in my room, I sat down for a while and tried to work out what I was going to say on a piece of paper. Despite what my mum thinks, I don't WANT to fall out with Goose. I really don't. She is the best friend I've ever had. On my piece of paper, I wrote:

<u>DON'T</u> give

Goose a

hard time!!!

But the more I tried to think about what I was actually going to say to her, the more muddled my head got and the more uptight I felt. Putting down my paper and pen, I lay on the floor for a bit and listened to some Jimi Hendrix songs on my MP3 player. I'd hoped that Jimi's voice would be a calming influence on me but, if anything, he just wound me up even more. After that, I tried listening to a bit of Beyoncé but I can't say that I found her particularly soothing either. She actually gave me a bit of a headache, if I'm honest.

Finally, I took a deep breath, selected Goose's number on my phone and pressed *Call*. While the call was connecting, I kept muttering 'Don't give Goose a hard time . . . Don't give Goose a hard time . . .' over and over so that I wouldn't forget.

'Hi, Lotts,' said Goose's voice in my ear. 'I'm just around the corner from your house. Shall I stop by?'

'NICE OF YOU TO TELL ME YOU'RE GOING OUT WITH SPUD,' I said. I didn't say it very nicely either.

There was a bit of a pause and then Goose said, 'I was going to tell you, Lottie. It's just that –'

'When?' I said. 'When exactly were you going to tell me?'

'Well, I would have told you this morning on the way to school,' said Goose. 'But when I called for you, you'd already left without me. What was that all about?'

Goose's voice was starting to sound a bit agitated.

'I just can't believe that you've been going out with Spud for a week – AN ENTIRE WEEK – and you didn't bother to tell me. I'm supposed to be your BEST FRIEND, Goose, but I had to hear about this from Gareth. And Gareth said that the ENTIRE SCHOOL knows. Everyone in Cardiff knows probably – except me. THANKS A LOT!'

I was crying now. I'd also screwed up the piece of paper which was advising me not to give Goose a hard time and thrown it into the bin under my desk.

On the other end of the phone, there was a long pause. Finally, Goose said, 'I've been meaning to phone you, actually, but . . .'

'But what?' I said.

There was another pause and then Goose said, 'But I've used all my credit talking to Spud.'

Confused, I said, 'But you could have just TOLD me! I was with you in town ALL AFTERNOON last week and you never said a word!'

Goose said, 'Will you STOP shouting at me, please?'

I said, 'I'm NOT shouting.'

Goose sort of laughed in my ear – although it wasn't a cheery laugh. Then she said, 'Well I'm sorry,' – although she didn't sound sorry – 'But how am I supposed to talk to you if you WON'T EVEN walk to school with me? THIS WEEK, the only time I've seen you is in English lessons and I'm hardly going to tell you intimate details about my private life in a poxy old English lesson, am I?'

Goose was sounding really REALLY agitated now. I think she was crying a bit too.

'Well, it's not MY FAULT if you'd rather hang around with Samantha Gorgon–Morgan, is it?' I shouted.[14]

'WHAT?' said Goose. 'WHAT?' She made a big angry noise in my ear and then said, 'Samantha Morgan's all right actually. Whatever your problem is with her, you need to get over it right now because SHE doesn't keep whining on about YOU every ten seconds. And at least I can have a PROPER conversation with her and tell her stuff about MY LIFE once in a while.'

'What's that supposed to mean?' I said.

'Ohhhh!' Goose made another big angry noise in my ear. 'I mean that I can have a two-way conversation with her. It's no wonder I never told you I fancied Spud. I never had the chance. Because it's always YOU YOU YOU. Except just recently when it's been YOU YOU YOU talking about GARETH GARETH GARETH.

---

[14] The Gorgon Sisters were these weird Greek women who had snakes on their heads instead of hair and were so ugly that any man who looked at them turned instantly to stone. To be strictly fair, Samantha Morgan isn't actually quite as bad as that.

You never listen, Lottie. You only ever talk. About yourself. You're probably not even listening to me now.'

I continued to hold the phone to my ear but only because all my brain cells had seized up and I'd gone into some kind of weird trance. My mouth was hanging open but not a single sound was coming out of it.

'Well it's true,' said Goose, a little bit quieter now and between big sniffs. I could tell she was DEFINITELY crying. 'You're bloody hard work sometimes and I've just about had enough of it.'

My brain couldn't quite believe what my left ear was hearing. Goose is supposed to be my very best friend in the whole world. I've always assumed we would be best friends forever. I even have this future image of us hanging out together, just being old. We go to The Jean Genie to each have a shampoo and set and then we have Pensioner's Portion lunches at the Dragon Coffee House before shuffling off to Vogue Marché to buy our matching culottes . . .

But instead of telling Goose any of this, I said, 'FINE. Then why don't you go and get yourself a new best friend.'

It wasn't a question. It was a statement and I shouted it at her. If I'd had something of Goose's that I could have thrown out of my window and broken, I would have done.

Goose said, 'OK, I will,' and then she switched her phone off.

And that's how she ended our friendship. As casually as that.

For a little while, I was a bit shocked. I just sat on the floor of my bedroom and wished that I could start the conversation all over again and do it differently. In the back of my head, there was a niggling voice which kept saying, 'Don't give Goose a hard time.'

I bit my thumbnail and said out loud, 'Whoops! I think I just did though.' And then I plugged my MP3 player into my speakers and listened to some Jimi Hendrix with the volume on maximum so any niggly voices would get totally drowned out.

And after a while, I stopped feeling bad and started feeling a bit annoyed with Goose. Because if things had been the other way round, I'd NEVER have agreed to go and find a new best friend as readily as she did. I value her friendship much more than that. It's like my mum said – she's not the sort of friend you can just go and order out of a catalogue. But CLEARLY Goose thinks she's got people queuing up round the block just waiting to step in and take my place. In fact, Samantha Gorgon-Morgan has probably elbowed her way right to the very front of the queue.

I read some more of that book *The Picture of Dorian Gray* which Mr Wood is forcing us to read. I picked it up out of sheer desperation because I needed something to take my mind off the fact that Goose is a colossal disappointment. It's quite heavy going because the author, Oscar Wilde, has a fantastically boring way of writing and keeps on deliberately using loads of complicated words just to show off. In spite of that, it's not entirely rubbish. Dorian Gray is actually extremely good-looking and everyone who knows him fancies him a bit – even the other men. I can relate to Oscar's story on a personal level because my ex-best friend Goose is also extremely good-looking and it wouldn't surprise me in the slightest to learn that the whole of Cardiff is secretly in love with her and wishes that they could marry her or at least be her next best friend or something. Come to think of it, it wouldn't actually surprise me to learn that Goose is secretly in love with herself.

Because she clearly thinks she's as tasty as chocolate.

seQuINs aND surPrIses

I'm really not that bothered about falling out with Goose. All I ever did was hang around her house from time to time and watch the *Free Willy* films back to back on DVD. Whereas now, Gareth comes over to mine and I get to snuggle up to him and watch films like *Legends of Welsh Rugby* and *England 19 – Wales 26*. Strictly speaking, I wouldn't normally choose to watch this kind of stuff because it just looks to me like a bunch of podgy, hairy men running about and bundling on top of each other. I can't honestly say that I get the point of it. But what I definitely DO understand is that these films become a BILLION times more interesting in Gareth's company because every time Wales score, he leaps to his feet, beats his chest like he's a gorilla, and then gives me a big smoochy pashy. It gives the game of rugby a whole new exciting dimension.

Although he only does this if my mum is out.

And anyway, my weekend is proving to be far too hectic to waste time worrying about Gail McKenzie and her hurtful comments. They were just words. *Mere Words! How terrible they were! How clear and vivid and cruel!*[15]

Goose's stupid words mean nothing compared to the exciting and interesting and *actual* things happening right now in my life.

---

[15] Actually, I have borrowed these lines from Oscar Wilde. I am up to page nineteen of his book now. I have another hundred and sixty-nine pages to go. ☺

Things like:

- My new job in the pumping heart of the glamour industry
- My new friends, Neil and Dilys
- My blossoming relationship with my future mother-in-law, Jean Stingecombe
- And definitely best of all – Winnie! But I'll say more about him later.

Yesterday was my first Saturday at The Jean Genie. I was actually really nervous when I woke up and I almost asked my mum if she'd ring in sick for me but then I remembered that:

    a)   There's no way she'd do it
and
    b) I wanted the cash.

I was really panicked about going in though so I sat inside my wardrobe for a while and started to think about what Blake might say to me in this situation. I know it sounds a bit weird to sit in a wardrobe but I've previously discovered that this is actually a very useful place for having a quiet moment. My wardrobe is fairly big and when I pull the door closed, it provides a very calm and peaceful environment to think in, even though it's a bit stuffy and I have to sit on a pile of shoes. But on this occasion, sitting on my shoes was definitely worth it because, all of a sudden, I could imagine Blake saying, 'What's the worst thing that could happen today, Lottie?' When I thought about it, I realized that the very *worst* that could happen was that Jean Stingecombe might give me the sack. And things didn't seem anywhere near as bad after that because I knew that this would mean I'd get to come home early and go back to bed.

When I arrived at the salon, it wasn't open and I could tell that nobody else was about yet because the door was still locked and there were no lights on inside. Jean had told me to be at the salon for half past nine. I bobbed down and leaned against the wall and looked at my watch.

It was 8.17.

I was OVER AN HOUR early. Mr Thomas, my double science teacher, once told me that some people believe that time is a fundamental constant and therefore can always be quantified according to a fixed measure. This sounds incredibly clever and complicated but actually it's a load of old twonk. I told Mr Thomas this. I said, 'I'm sorry, Mr T, but that's a load of total old twonk. I happen to know for a fact that there is *definitely* nothing constant or fixed about time. Sometimes, a single minute in my life can feel like it's taking forever and other times, like when I'm watching *X Factor* or when I'm in the bath, ages and ages can slip past really quickly without me even realizing it.'

Mr Thomas had then smiled in a meaningful and intellectual manner and launched into some boring complicated waffle that went along these lines:

'Well observed, Lottie. But I never said that *I* support this notion of time being fixed. This is *obviously* a pre-relativistic version of time and not one that our good friend Mr Einstein would agree with. Scientific theory has moved *far* beyond such a simple definition. But if you really want to learn more about this, I can lend you some very interesting magazine articles on the subject.'

'No, you're OK,' I said.

'Oh, and I'd prefer it if you didn't call me Mr T.'

He's a nice enough man but he does talk a colossal amount of scatty crap sometimes.

But the point I am trying to make is that TIME IS BLATANTLY AS STRETCHY AS BUBBLEGUM and even Albert Einstein, the great scientific expert, would agree with me on this matter. Most Saturday mornings, I barely have time to get up, eat something and watch a bit of telly before it starts getting dark again. So it was a total and utter head shock when I looked down at my watch as I crouched uncomfortably outside the salon. I'd already been awake for ages and yet my watch was telling me that it was *still* an anti-social hour. I really wished it had occurred to me to check it before I left the house.

At seven minutes past nine, Jean rocked up. She said, 'Hiya, lovely. You're bright and early. Have you been waiting long?'

I stood up and said, 'About an hour.' There were pins and needles in my feet and I was staggering around a bit on the pavement because I'd lost control of my lower limbs.

Jean gave me a funny look and then said, 'Well, there's nothing like being early, is there?'

'Not really,' I said. 'It's unique.' To be honest, I was just making small talk.

Jean unlocked the door and we went inside and she made me a cup of coffee. 'It's just as well you're here in good time, Lottie, my love,' she said as she handed me my mug. 'It'll give you an opportunity to get a feel for your new uniform.'

'Uniform?' I said, and frowned a bit. Apart from a stint as a baton-twirler in the Pontypridd Majorette Troop, I've never really enjoyed wearing any sort of uniform – and I didn't wear that one for very long. I was only a member for a couple of months in Year 9. My mum quickly got fed up with driving me all the way to Ponty for rehearsals and I quickly got fed up with people at school hilariously asking me if I'd had PMT last night.

'That's right, Lottie, my love,' said Jean. 'I run a tight ship here and it's important that we're all identifiable as members of the same crew.'

And then she handed me a dodgy black T-shirt with silver sequins sewn on it in flowery patterns and a pair of matching culottes. I quietly went to the staff toilet and put them on. I didn't even object a tiny bit. Not even slightly. And even though my mum thinks that Goose is the bee's knees and the kitten's mittens, I'd be prepared to bet all the money that I've ever touched in my entire life that Goose would NEVER have worn those culottes as quietly and as maturely as I did!

Not that I actually care what Goose would have done anyway.

When I came back from the toilet, Dilys was in the salon pulling hair out of her brushes and chatting to Jean. Of course, she was wearing the same clothes as me. Side by side, I suppose we must have looked like this:

When Dilys saw me she said, 'Ooh hello, Lottie, love. You and me look like two peas in a pod, don't we? Do you think the clients will be able to tell us apart?'

'I doubt it,' I said and then I burst out laughing because, actually, I think we looked nothing like each other.

Dilys beamed back at me and said, 'Ooh, haven't you got a lovely little face when you laugh?' Then she turned to Jean Stingecombe and said, 'Hasn't Lottie got a lovely little face when she's laughing?'

Jean said, 'She's got an adorable little face. I can see exactly why she managed to catch the eye of a big handsome boy like my Gazzy.'

Dilys said, 'Ooh Lottie, you've done well there, my lovely. He's a great big hunk of chunk is your Gazzy.'

Jean said, 'Stop it, Dilys. You'll be making Lottie get all jealous.'

'Ooh, if I were fifty years younger I'd fight her for him,' said Dilys.

'Behave yourself, young lady,' said Jean to Dilys, and then she said to me, 'Are we embarrassing you, my lovely?'

It's hard to know quite what to say in a situation like this. A voice inside my head was screaming,

'URGGHHH . . . YUCK . . .

STOP IT . . .
SHUT UP . . .'

But it didn't really seem appropriate to tell my current boss and future mother-in-law to shut up so I just laughed again and said, 'Um . . . sort of.'

And we all laughed again and then a mad alien walked through the door of the salon and said, 'Hello.'

And that made me do this:

A Shocked pose!

Dilys said, 'Ooh, here comes handsome.'

Jean said, 'Hiya, Neil, love.'

And I said nothing at all because I was too shocked.

'Lottie, this is Neil,' said Jean. 'He's our Trainee Stylist.'

And Neil looked at me and said, 'Hi. I think I know you, don't I?'

I nodded and went red. I knew exactly who Neil was – even if he seemed to have completely forgotten who *I* was. He was none other than

Neil Adam

who used to go out with my ex-best friend Goose before he cheated on her and then dumped her via a text message. And back then, he had – and still has now – ridiculously beautiful cheekbones. And his name backwards is Mad Alien, which is atrociously stupid of his parents when you stop and think about it. And after he dumped Goose, she and I decided that we'd never EVER speak to him again.

But that was when she was still my best friend.

'Hi, Neil,' I said and gave him my biggest and friendliest smile. 'I didn't know you worked here.'

'One day I'm going to have a whole chain of top-class salons called *Hair by Neil Adam*,' said Neil Adam. And then he sucked in his cheeks so his cheekbones stuck out even more and looked all gorgeous.

'Wow!' I said.

'Now now, Lottie,' said Jean. 'Don't you go getting too pally-pally with my handsome Trainee Stylist. Just you remember that you're going out with the boss's son!'

'Ooh, and anyway,' said Dilys with a cheeky wink at Neil, 'Neily-Weily's only got eyes for me. Ain't that right, Neily, my love.'

'Certainly is, Dilys,' said Neil with a cheeky wink straight back at her. To me, he added, 'No offence, Lottie, but you just aren't my type.' Then he unzipped his coat to reveal that he *too* was wearing a shiny black sequinned T-shirt. It fitted him so snugly that I could see the outline of his muscles very clearly. And even though I am blatantly IN LOVE WITH GARETH, I have to say that Neil Adam aka Mad Alien[16] does have a very impressive upper body. Gareth has got bigger thighs though. Mercifully, instead of our matching culottes, Neil was wearing his sequinned top with a pair of regular black trousers. He still looked a bit strange though. I don't think I'd like to see Gareth in sequins. But Jean runs a tight ship at The Jean Genie so it's really very important that we all look like members of the same crew. Neil is obviously mature enough to realize this.

There's no way Goose would be.

Not that I care.

Like I said, I'm not that bothered about falling out with her.

---

[16] This is totally and utterly a palindrome.

At half past four, just as Neil was sweeping up the last reminders of Mrs Owen's dreadful – but now, thankfully, departed – mahogany beehive, Jean Stingecombe locked the door of the salon and hung the *Closed* sign in the window.

'We're shutting the salon early today, team,' she said, '. . . for some staff development.'

I put down the *Hair Necessities* magazine I'd been reading for the past hour and said, 'What's that?' I was genuinely interested. I've never worked anywhere that develops staff before.

'Training,' said Jean. 'I run a tight ship here. It's important that my crew are all familiar with the latest innovations in the industry.'

Dilys said, 'Ooh, whose hair are we experimenting on today, Jee? Neil's or Lottie's?'

'*Huh?*' I said. '*Huh?*' And then, after an uneasy pause in which I ran my hand nervously over my ultra-modern Ancient Egyptian bob, I added, 'I don't want my hair cut, thanks. I'm happy with it as it is.'

Jean looked at me thoughtfully and said, 'Well, Lottie, you *are* the new recruit so we *will* need to restyle you a teensy-weensy bit. Ideally, your hair should be a reflection of the kind of image we aim to offer to our clients here at the salon.'

'But I don't want to look like an old person,' I said in a great big rushy panic.

'Ooh, hark at you!' said Dilys. 'You're only as old as the feller you're feeling. Ain't that right, Neily, my love?' And then she gave Neil a cheeky wink and playfully squeezed his biceps.

'Dilys, you're a sexual terrorist,' said Neil and then he made a growling noise as if he were a tiger and snarled at her in a deliberately suggestive manner.

Dilys chuckled happily and waddled off to the staffroom to fetch us all some mint humbugs.

I felt a bit sick. I don't know if it was because:

a) I DO NOT LIKE sexy jokes
b) My Ancient Egyptian bob was feeling threatened

or

c) I'd helped Dilys to munch her way through three bags of mint humbugs already.

'But I don't want my hair cut,' I said again. I was starting to feel quite agitated and my cheeks had gone all hot. If I'd had a wardrobe handy, I'd have gratefully climbed into it.

'It's all right,' said Neil with a shrug and a nod at Jean, 'I'll do it.' He glanced at himself in the mirror and added, 'Can you give me something a bit choppy on top, feathery at the sides and ragged at the back? And maybe you could cut into it so that it looks slightly more textured and a little less heavy. And perhaps try to bring out my cinnamon lowlights a bit more. Whatever you do, don't use the clippers though!'

'Neily, you're an absolute angel,' said Jean and blew a kiss which Neil pretended to catch.

Dilys returned with a new bag of mint humbugs and mumbled something about her varicose veins playing up.

'Positions then, team,' said Jean. 'Lottie, come and stand over here with Dilys and watch the way I rework Neil's hair.'

And then Jean began chopping and feathering and ragging Neil's hair, and while she snipped, she sang '*Yoo-hoo make me feeeeel, yoo-hoo make me feeeel, yoo-hoo make me feeeeeeeel like an act-u-al wo-man,*' along to the song which was coming out of the salon's speakers and had, in fact, been coming out of the salon's speakers more or less all day.

When she'd finished, she put down her scissors and stood back to admire her handiwork. Neil Adam aka Mad Alien looked not entirely dissimilar to this:

Which just goes to prove, without any shadow of a doubt, that my future mother-in-law, Jean Stingecombe, is a supremely brilliant stylist and Neil Adam is EXTRAORDINARILY attractive. I know that sounds a bit disloyal to my Gareth but I can't entirely help it. Just like that woman in the song, I'm an *actual woman* and sometimes – just occasionally – I have to acknowledge that I have an actual woman's urges.

After my staff development, I walked home in a good mood. Looking back on it all, I am now extremely glad that I never asked my mum to phone in sick for me. It might have seemed like the easiest thing to do at the time but it wouldn't really have done me any favours in the long term. Sometimes it's better to just confront certain sensitive situations head on. And by getting up and getting on with it, I've been rewarded with several new and interesting pieces of information to help me on my journey through life. I've written them all down in a list.

New and Interesting Things I Learned Yesterday

1. Neil Adam aka Mad Alien may once have dumped Gail Mckenzie via a text message but that does not stop him from actually being a very pleasant person.

2. According to several clientele of The Jean Genie, I have a nice telephone voice.

3. White towels are for regular use and navy towels are for clients who are having a colour application.

4. Earl Grey tea is usually made without any milk.

5. Clients like it when you press their head during a shampooing.
6. They also love it if you ask them about their holidays.

It may not seem like a huge list but, as a general rule, I don't usually learn this many new and interesting things on an average school day.

And then when I got home, my day got even better. My mum was keeping a lookout for me from the living room window and as soon as she saw me walking down our road, she waved and rushed off to open the front door.

'Day OK?' she asked.

'Not bad,' I said.

'Gareth's mum all right?' she asked.

'Seemed OK,' I said.

'Learn anything interesting?' she asked.

'Nah,' I said.

And then she flapped her hands about in front of her and said really loudly,

'I can't keep it from you any longer. I've got you a chinchilla. Come and have a look at him.'

And I said,

'Oh my God! That's totally amazing! I love chinchillas so much. I can't believe you've actually seriously gone and got me one. Where is he?'

And then we both went rushing off to the kitchen to check out my chinchilla. I was so excited that I almost puked.

My chinchilla was sitting on the kitchen table inside a massive cage which had several different levels and a little tray at the bottom filled with fine sand. He was perched up on the highest level and appeared to be asleep. I leaned forward to get a better view of him. He looked a bit odd. I leaned forward even closer and examined him again.

My mum said, 'Do you like him?'

I looked at the little animal which was fast asleep in front of me. Like the chinchillas in Happy Pets, he was round and furry with a pointy nose and chicken feet but that was where any similarity ended. I'd never seen any living thing quite like this one ever before. My chinchilla was round but not very fat with enormously long whiskers and grubby white fur. He was just like a scruffy fluffy snowball. I put my hand in the cage and gently prodded him. He lifted his head to look at me and then shifted about a bit before curling up into a sleepy ball again. He seemed to be a bit doddery on his feet, if I'm honest.

I said, 'What's the matter with him?'

My mum went a bit red and said, 'Well . . . nothing. He's just old.'

'Why did you get me such an ancient one?' I said.

My mum went even redder and said, 'Well, they're not cheap, you know, Lottie. I looked in the pet shop and a young chinchilla was ninety pounds. That's a lot more than a rabbit costs.'

I continued to watch my ancient chinchilla. I could see his body move up and down as he was breathing.

'And also, did you know that a chinchilla can live for over twenty years?' added my mum. 'That means that if I'd bought you a baby, you might still have been looking after him well into your late thirties. That's a *serious* commitment. I thought maybe we should see how we get on with this old sweetie first.'

My ancient chinchilla blinked open an eye and then gave a sleepy yawn before nodding off again.

'I'd planned to call him Hendrix,' I said. 'After Jimi Hendrix. But I'm not sure that the name Hendrix really suits this particular chinchilla.'

'Well, actually, he's already got a name,' said my mum. 'He's called Winnie. I got him out of the local paper. His owner couldn't look after him any more.'

I put my hand back inside the cage and ran a finger across

Winnie's head. His fur was the softest thing I've ever felt. It's exactly the same texture as crushed velvet. Winnie wiggled his ears and made a funny little chirping sound.

'Do you like him?' said my mum again. She sounded a bit worried. I don't know why though.

'I LOVE HIM,' I said with a big smile. 'He is totally *totally* lush.'

And then I gave my mum a big hug and shortly after that, Gareth rang me up to see how I'd got on at his mum's salon, and later today, he's coming around to tea and bringing a film called *The Official History of Welsh Rugby* with him. So I'm having Sunday afternoon with a hunk of chunk and a chinchilla.

What more could a girl possibly want?

I am in a state of

total and utter

trauma.

So terrible is my condition that I've had to take a day off school. My mum thinks I've got a migraine but actually the truth is far more serious. An unfortunate chain of events has forced me to undertake a terrible journey of self-discovery and that terrible journey has made me arrive at a very shocking and concerning conclusion.

I want to do *it* with Gareth Stingecombe.

I want to do *it* so badly that I'm in danger of becoming desperate. It's a very difficult thing to accept about myself. To make matters even worse, the one person I would normally turn to for guidance and advice at such a moment of personal crisis is Goose and, unfortunately, she is unavailable for comment because I shouted at her and told her to go and get a new best friend. Sometimes, I am colossally stupid. Friends like Goose McKenzie are hard to find. You can't just go and order one out of a catalogue.

I've got Jimi Hendrix to thank for ultimately showing me the alarming truth. I always knew that there was a hidden depth to Jimi's music but now I know that it has the power to unlock parts of my brain that I never even knew existed. But I also have Oscar Wilde to thank. And Winnie the chinchilla too. On Sunday, I moved Winnie's cage into my bedroom because I thought he seemed a bit lonely in the kitchen and I have since discovered that Winnie is *not* the quiet little creature that he at first appeared to be. All day, while I'm at school, he sleeps in a little wooden box inside his massive cage, and all night, while I'm in bed, he bounces about like a ping-pong ball and keeps me awake.

Without this interruption to my nightly sleep patterns, I might never have realized quite how desperately I want to have intimate physical contact with Gareth Stingecombe's body.

It's Friday now and Winnie has been living in my bedroom for five days. I haven't had a decent kip in all that time. The first night the bouncing happened was Sunday and I just put it down to a bit of overexcitement. Gareth had been over at my house showing me his rugby DVD and then we'd gone upstairs to my bedroom partly so that I could show him Winnie but mostly so that I could have a bit of privacy with Gareth away from the undercover police surveillance of my mum. When he'd seen Winnie, Gareth had poked him with his finger and said, 'I'm not being funny but he doesn't do much, does he?'

'Shut up,' I'd said. 'You'll hurt his feelings. He's a very elderly chinchilla and at this time of his life he just wants to take it easy and relax. He doesn't want some great big hunk of chunk like you prodding him about and being all critical.'

'Sorry,' Gareth said. And then he leaned over so that his face was level with Winnie's face and said, 'Sorry, Winnie.'

Winnie made a chirping noise and shut his eyes.

Gareth straightened up and said, 'I've got some amazing new bruises that I picked up on the field of play, Lottie. I've got this massive big blue one on my thigh and all the rugby boys reckon that it looks *exactly* like Marge Simpson. Do you want to see it?'

Now normally I would have no interest in looking at bruises but the location of this particular one made it more fascinating than most. I nodded gormlessly.

Gareth said, 'Your mum won't come bursting in here, will she?'

Still totally devoid of any gorms, I shook my head. My mouth had suddenly gone all dry and I wasn't sure if I could speak.

Gareth put his finger on his lips to tell me to keep quiet and then undid the belt of his jeans. I sat down on my bed and tried to look normal. It was really hard though because my face muscles were freaking out.

Gareth looked anxiously at the door and then lowered his jeans so that they were just above his knees.

'Yuck!' I said, really loudly. 'You're wearing Britney Spears boxer shorts!'

And then I blushed really furiously because it suddenly occurred to me that I happened to be wearing my lucky Justin Timberlake knickers.[17]

Gareth blushed really furiously too and looked down at his pants. Then he shrugged his shoulders and said, 'Oh, these aren't mine. I accidentally tipped a can of cola into my undies drawer and all my boxers had to be washed. I nicked these ones off my dad.' Then he pointed at a big blue blob on his thigh and said, 'There it is! It's really enormous, isn't it?'

I gulped and said, 'Wow! It really is. It's huge!'

And it was. It took my breath away just looking at it.

And what's more, it *did* sort of look like Marge Simpson.

Gareth pulled his jeans up with a proud smile and then sat down on the bed next to me. 'Coach Jenkins reckons I've got a good chance of making it as a regular in the Wales youth team.' His eyes were locked on mine.

---

[17] I can't decide whether this is a sign of our total compatibility or of an absolute love disaster.

'That's amazing, Gaz,' I replied. My eyes were locked on his.

'Coach Jenkins reckons I've got the makings of a great scrum-half,' said Gareth. His face was moving ever so slowly towards my face.

'I'm sure you have,' I murmured back. I was suddenly breathing like somebody who was in the middle of a cross-country race.

Gareth put his hands on my waist and whispered, 'Coach Jenkins reckons—'

'Oh, Gaz, will you shut up about Coach Jenkins?' I said. And Gareth nodded his head furiously and fell forwards and then our lips met in an explosion of passion and lust and Gareth pushed me back on to my bed and clambered a bit on top of me and covered me with urgent little fiery kisses and my hands were on his waist and then on his belt and I could feel that his jeans were still undone and –

THUD

Gareth sat up sharply. 'What was that noise?'

THUD

'What noise?' I said. 'I didn't hear anything.'

THUD

'*That* noise,' said Gareth, and I sat up then because I couldn't realistically pretend to ignore it any more.

THUD

'It's Winnie,' said Gareth. 'He's woken up!'

I smoothed down my top because it had got all creased up in the scrum and then I turned to look at Winnie and he was doing this:

'He might be old,' said Gareth, 'but he's bouncy.'

I bit my thumbnail and said, 'Yeah, but can we just go back to where we were a minute ago?'

Gareth laughed and pulled a face. 'Don't seem right really, Lottie. Not in front of an elderly chinchilla.' And then he punched me playfully on the arm and said, 'Let's go and play *Super Mario Karts* with your mum. I still haven't got over the fact that she beat me the other day. Honestly, it's doing my head in. The rugby boys would kill themselves laughing if they ever found out.'

And that was where my journey of frustration started.

After Gareth had gone home, I went straight back up to my bedroom. For a while, I just paced around unsure of what to do with myself and then, finally, I climbed into bed with all my clothes still on. It was only a little after seven and way too early to be in bed, dressed or not. Probably my little brother, Caradoc, doesn't even go to bed that early and he's only five! Mind you, I wouldn't know when his bedtime is because he lives in Wrexham and that's miles away. Downstairs, I could hear my mum crashing about and laughing as she did her step aerobics in front of the telly. Just recently, we've been doing this together because Blake reckons it's good for us. This time, though, there was *no way* that I was going to prance about like a pillock in front of my mum. I didn't even want to be anywhere near her. To be honest, I was worried that she'd take one look at me and be able to see right inside my filthy head and know what I was thinking.

I'm not going into detail about what I *was* thinking about because it makes me too flustered.

I'll leave it as a complete mystery.

So instead of prancing about like a pillock with my mum, I lay in my bed, fully clothed, and stared at the ceiling for a while. Winnie was bouncing around in his cage and making a right old racket. 'Thanks, Winnie,' I whispered crossly. 'Things were starting to get really interesting in my bedroom for a moment there. And then you had to wake up and ruin it all.'

Winnie winked at me and made his sweet little chirping noise. I felt a bit bad then. After all, it wasn't really Winnie's fault that I was feeling weird. And it's totally wrong to get annoyed with an animal. Everyone knows that.

'Sorry, Winnie,' I said. 'But I'm a bit wound up.'

Winnie chirped again and then leaped up to the top of his cage. He seemed quite happy with his new set-up. I watched him jump about for a while and then, because I was still being tormented by dodgy mental images, I picked up that Oscar Wilde book and stared at the cover for a bit. This worked a treat. Within minutes, all dodgy mental images had left my head and I was feeling so bored that I put my light out and went to sleep. Even though it wasn't even eight o'clock.

But the next night, Winnie started bouncing again. And while he bounced, I couldn't sleep. And as I couldn't sleep, I started thinking. And the only single thing I could think about was that very same dodgy mental picture – which may, or may not, have involved a pair of Britney Spears boxer shorts – and this got me feeling agitated all over again.

So I picked up Oscar Wilde's book again and this time I actually opened it and started reading and I read until my eyes were aching and I could hardly find the energy to switch off my reading lamp. And then I went through the exact same process the next night. And the next. *And* the next. And now it's Friday and I'm on page one hundred and sixty-eight already and I haven't actually got all that much more left to read! And it's really not a bad book because it's about this man who stays young and beautiful while his portrait gets more old and ugly with each terrible and atrocious thing that he does. But while I was lying in bed and reading all this, the thing that *really* fascinated me was not so much this story but something that Oscar Wilde had written way back near the beginning. No matter how much further I read on, I just kept returning each night to this page and re-reading the words I'd found there.

> *The only way to get rid of a temptation is to yield to it. Resist it, and your soul grows sick with longing for the things it has forbidden itself.*

And I wasn't one hundred per cent certain what it all meant but I couldn't get it out of my brain. It felt as if Oscar was speaking directly to me right from the page and he was advising me to do something. And I had the distinct impression that what he was advising me to do was something that I probably totally shouldn't.

aND theN I sPOke tO GOOse

This week hasn't been one of my best. I'm feeling as edgy as an eggshell. If you must know, I've currently got more edge than Australia and according to my geography teacher that's got more than 16,000 miles of edge. So I'm **seriously very edgy**. I suppose it's hardly surprising. I've been on the receiving end of some **extreme** mental torment.

Even the most rock solid person in the whole of Rock-Solid-Land would be feeling a bit wobbly if they were in my position.

Yesterday, when I went downstairs for my breakfast, my mum was in the kitchen. She was sitting at the table reading a newspaper and drinking coffee. When she saw me, she put down her paper and said, 'Is Goose calling round for you this morning?'

'No,' I said.

My mum took a sip of her coffee and looked at me all thoughtfully as if I'd just said something incredibly complicated. I tipped a load of Choco Pops into a bowl and waited for her to speak again. I knew she'd have more to say. She had her police interrogation face on.

'I haven't seen Goose for a while. Is everything OK?'

'Yep,' I said and sploshed milk over my cereal. My shoulders had gone all tense. I knew she still hadn't finished.

My mum frowned. Then, after a massive pause, she said, 'I haven't heard you mention Goose since you had that private telephone conversation with her. You didn't give her a hard time, did you?'

'NO,' I said.

My mum frowned again and had another sip of her coffee. 'But you're not walking to school with her these days?'

'Nope,' I said.

'But everything's OK between you?'

I shrugged and then shovelled a deliberately large spoonful of cereal into my mouth so that I was unable to speak without spitting Choco Pops at her.

My mum said, 'Ruthie phoned me last night to say she's coming home for the weekend and she's bringing a friend, Michelle, with her. I thought it might be fun if we invite Goose over on Saturday evening and have a *Mamma Mia!* night. I could make some popcorn and the five of us could have a girly night in. What do you reckon?'

I stopped munching my Choco Pops and looked at her

in horror. It was, without a doubt, one of the most tragic ideas I'd ever heard in my entire life. I love my sister Ruthie very much[18] but I don't want to sing rotten old Abba songs in front of her. I don't want to sing Abba songs in front of anyone. And I don't want a girly night in with my mum. And Goose wouldn't come anyway because I shouted at her down the phone. I couldn't be bothered to explain all of this to my mum though, so instead, I forced down my Choco Pops and said, 'I can't. I've already made a prior engagement with Gareth.'

My mum frowned. 'Can't you change your plans for this one night? Just while Ruthie is home? I'm sure Gareth'll understand.'

'Nope,' I said. 'He's taking me to see *Shark Mutilation 3* at the cinema. He's already bought the tickets.'

He wasn't and he hadn't. I'd just made it up.

My mum frowned again and said, 'That's a shame. I really fancied some time with the girls. Maybe Goose could come over and have some Sunday lunch with us instead?'

'Nope,' I said, 'Gareth's mum has invited me to their house for Sunday lunch.'

She hadn't. I'd just made that up as well.

My mum narrowed her eyes and looked at me in the kind of way that only someone who is a Detective Sergeant in the police force can do. Sort of like this:

---

[18] Well, a bit. Sometimes. When she's asleep. Or in Aberystwyth.

Before I continue, I should just clarify something. My mum doesn't have a moustache. She actually has a very smooth face. All the women in our family have always had very smooth faces. None of us have ever had a *ms*-tache. My mum doesn't smoke a pipe either. Or wear a Sherlock Holmes hat. In fact, this picture is much more representative of her *manner* than her actual physical appearance.

My mum said, 'I'm glad you're getting on so well with Gareth but don't forget the rest of us, will you.'

I shovelled another large spoonful of Choco Pops into my mouth.

My mum looked at the clock, stood up and put her coffee cup into the sink. 'I have to be off,' she said. 'Have a good day and say hello to Goose for me.'

I shrugged, munched my Choco Pops and grunted.

Just as my mum was about to leave the kitchen, she paused and said, 'How are you getting on with Winnie in your room? Somebody at work told me that chinchillas can be very active at night. He's not keeping you awake, is he?'

I swallowed my cereal really quickly and said, 'No way! He's as quiet as a mouse. I don't hear a peep out of him.'

I'm not sure why I said this. Winnie is, after all, causing me serious sleep deprivation. At the end of the day, I suppose this lie proves that I like having his bouncy little presence in my bedroom.

But it was still about the billionth lie I'd told in the space of five minutes. I gave my mum a quick smile and tried to look like an honest and trustworthy person even though I was actually starting to remind myself of that terrible Dorian Gray character in my English reading book. He was a dodgy little liar as well. If I had a portrait of myself hidden away in some disused bedroom, it would probably be looking quite old and ugly by now.

My mum smiled and said, 'Good old Winnie,' and then she picked up her coat and bag, blew me a kiss and left.

I put my cereal bowl into the sink and picked up my own bag. All through Year 10 I was using a genuine authentic Donna Karan handbag for school, but this year, I have gone very minimalist and anti-capitalist and I'm refusing to use anything except a plastic Nike carrier bag which I got given for free when I bought my last pair of bling new limited-edition trainers. I think it makes me look as if I'm stylish without even trying to be. Next, I pushed my earphones into my ears, dropped my MP3 player into the pocket of my trousers, grabbed my keys and set off on the short walk to school. I didn't bother with a coat. To be honest, I *never* bother to wear a coat if my mum has left the house before me. Coats are for softies.

At the school gates, I saw Samantha Morgan and Lee Fogel eating each other for breakfast. I'm surprised that those two have got any lips left. As I walked past them, Samantha Morgan must have opened her eyes long enough to spot me because she called out, 'Oi, Lottie! Go and talk to Goose. She's really upset, you know.'

I paused for a second and then I said, 'Yeah, so am I!'

Lee Fogel smirked and said, 'That's not exactly news, is it, Potty?' And then he turned his back on me and buried his teeth in Samantha's neck. I pretended to chuck up in front of them and walked on through the gates, but as I did, I heard Samantha mouthing off in an angry voice behind me. I turned and opened my mouth to yell something back at her but then I hesitated and closed it again. She wasn't shouting at me. She wasn't even looking in my direction. Lee had stopped slobbering all over her and they were having some sort of argument instead.

It got me thinking about Goose though. It got me thinking again about how stupid I was to go around upsetting her. I know she's quite irritating sometimes. And I know that she's a bit too pretty and annoyingly popular and aggravatingly clever and blood-boilingly brilliant at absolutely everything. And I know, too, that she definitely *does* think that she's as tasty as chocolate. But she's still the coolest person that I've ever met. And she *did* sit around my house with me all summer while I was recovering from my reasonably significant mental disturbance. And if the Prime Minister said to me, 'Lottie, you've GOT to sit through a *Mamma Mia!* night with your mum and your sister because it's the LAW', then I'd DEFINITELY want Goose to be there to go through it all with me. Because, after all, she's fab. I suppose I just need to be a bit nicer to her sometimes and stop being such a crabby old witch.

So right there and then, I decided that as soon as I had the chance, I'd apologize to Goose and ask her if we could be friends again. My first lesson was English and me and Goose share the same desk so I knew I wouldn't have very long to wait. As I walked to my registration room, I tried to work out what I was going to say to her. The prospect of apologizing was making me feel a bit nervous, to be honest. It's weird because I'm really good at saying what I want to say when I write stuff down but when I have to speak things out loud, I sometimes make a right nasty mess of it.

My brain was still whirring round with all this stuff when I walked straight smack bump into a couple of corridor snoggers.

'Watch where you're going!' said Goose, angrily, once

she'd detached herself from Spud's face. And then she went bright red and said, 'Oh, Lottie, it's you.'

I didn't know what to say. I rubbed my bumped shoulder and shrugged and then said, 'Oh yeah, so it is!' Looking back on it, I think I might have sounded slightly sarcastic.

Goose said, 'Are you OK?'

'Yep,' I said.

Spud smiled at me and then slipped his arm over Goose's shoulders.

Goose said, 'Look, Lottie, I'm sorry about the other day.'

Spud was looking bored and stroking Goose's left shoulder. I wished he'd just go away.

'I'm sorry too,' I said. 'It was my fault. I shouldn't have given you such a hard time on the phone.'

Goose grinned and looked relieved. 'It's all right, Lotts. Forget about it. Why don't you come over to my house on Saturday and watch a documentary I've got about the making of the *Free Willy* films? It seems like ages since we've done anything together.'

I laughed. 'No, I've got a better idea,' I said. And I was right on the very verge of telling her about my mum's poxy plan to have a *Mamma Mia!* party when I suddenly spotted something on Goose's neck which made me momentarily lose the ability to speak.

She had a dirty great love bite on her neck the size of Sexas. I mean Texas.

My cheeks had gone hot. Spud was still getting in the

way and draping himself all over Goose's shoulders. I tried to give him a look of blatant disapproval but suddenly all I could see was that vision of Gareth in his dad's Britney Spears boxer shorts. I felt my face go even hotter. Before I could stop myself, I opened my mouth and blurted out, 'I've got a better idea. Why don't I go and see *Shark Mutilation 3* at the cinema with Gareth?'

Goose stopped smiling and looked a bit confused.

'Because he's asked me and he's already bought the tickets,' I added, to try and make things better.

Goose gave me a puzzled smile and said, 'Oh. OK then.'

From somewhere further down the corridor, a familiar voice boomed out, 'Biggsy!'

It was Gareth. The vision of the BSBS flashed across my mind again. My cheeks were so hot I thought that I was about to spontaneously combust on the spot.

Gareth gave me a big bear hug from behind and kissed me on the cheek.

Spud said, 'All right, Stingey? So you're taking Lottie to see *Shark Mutilation 3* then? Nice one. Richard Pritchard told me that you actually get to see someone's head popping in that film.'

It was Gareth's turn to look confused. 'What are you on about?' he said.

Spud said, 'Lottie just said you're taking her to see the film on Saturday.'

Gareth looked even more perplexed and said, 'Am I? First I've heard about it.'

I could feel Goose staring at me. She'd gone a very deep purple colour. She looked as if she might be about to spontaneously combust as well.

'Remember?' I said to Gareth. 'Remember you said we'd go this Saturday?'

'Huh?' said Gareth.

I put my thumbnail in my mouth and bit on it. Goose hadn't taken her eyes off me. For a moment, I thought she looked a bit sad but when she spoke she just sounded plain furious. 'Got a better idea then, Lottie? Well, that's really nice. Thank you so much for making that abundantly clear.' And then she grabbed hold of Spud's hand and dragged him off down the corridor.

Gareth said, 'Er . . . have I done something wrong?'

I chewed my thumbnail and watched Goose disappear around the corner. 'No,' I sighed. 'But I have.' And then I grabbed hold of his hand and dragged him off to registration with me.

aND theN JImI heNDrIX askeD me the CrItICaL QuestION

In English, me and Goose didn't speak to each other. We just sat there, as serious as a couple of chess players, and pretended to be really interested in what Mr Wood was saying about the Oscar Wilde book.

'Has anyone read as far as page sixteen yet?' he asked the class in his foghorn voice.

I put my hand up and said, 'I'm up to page one hundred and sixty-two.'

Next to me, Goose muttered something and started scratching the desk with her thumbnail.

Mr Wood smiled and said, 'That's marvellous, Lottie. See! Didn't I tell you that you'd enjoy it? It's full of so many great and memorable quotations from the witty Mr Wilde. Are there any pearls of wisdom which have jumped out at you?'

I flicked to page nineteen and read out the words which I'd underlined there. '*The only way to get rid of a temptation is to yield to it.*'

Mr Wood said, 'Ah yes. One of Oscar Wilde's most famous lines. But is it good advice, Lottie?'

I shifted in my seat uncomfortably and said, 'How the heck should I know?'

Mr Wood's eyes twinkled back at me and he said, 'Indeed, how would you? I'm sure there is little in the way of temptation to trouble your lovely young mind.'

As soon as he said this, the BSBS popped into my head again. For the eighty-six millionth time in the space of five days, I felt my face get hot. I looked down at my desk and hoped Mr Wood couldn't see the terrible contents of my lovely young mind.

Mr Wood said, 'And how about you, Miss McKenzie? Have any of Oscar Wilde's words proved to be of particular interest to you?'

I sensed Goose's body give an ever so slight jump. She probably hadn't been expecting Mr Wood to start bending her brain as well. If I know Goose, she'd probably been composing some hit song lyrics in her head. I sat back in my chair and waited with interest for her response. My guess was that she'd been too busy receiving love bites from Spud to have actually started reading the book yet.

I was wrong though. Goose said, 'Yeah. This bit.' She picked up her book and read out loud, *'Some day you will look at your friend, and he will seem to you to be a little out of drawing, or you won't like his tone of colour or something.'* She slapped the book down on her desk and added, 'That line says a lot really, doesn't it?'

'Does it?' said Mr Wood.

'Yeah,' said Goose. 'It really sums up the *total disappointment* that you can feel when you realize that someone you *really* thought of as a good friend has changed and, actually, you see that they're *not* the fantastic person that you thought they were.'

Mr Wood put his head on one side and said, 'Hmmm,

interesting! Although I'm not sure that your interpretation is *quite* what Wilde actually intended. What do other people think?'

And then he asked the rest of the class for their opinions but, of course, no one actually had any because they were all in the very advanced stages of Death by Boredom. Beca Bowen was so far gone that she was even plucking her eyebrows. Goose shifted a bit in her seat so that she was looking out of the window and then went right back to scratching the desk with her thumbnail.

And I felt WORSE THAN EVER because I knew that Goose hadn't really been talking about that stupid book at all. She'd been talking about me.

Art was just as bad. Mr Spanton made us draw self-portraits using little mirrors that we had to hold out in front of us with one hand while we tried to sketch our own faces with another. I did my best but, really, I don't think my heart was in it. When I'd finished, Mr Spanton came over to have a look at what I'd done. Scratching his chin, he said, 'As an illustration, it's not without merit, Lottie. In fact, I suppose, we could argue that it's actually rather *avant-garde*.'

'Which means?' I asked.

'It's highly original. Definitely one of your more unique and innovative compositions. *However . . .*'

'However?' I asked.

'*However,*' repeated Mr Spanton, 'I did ask you to draw a *realistic* portrait of yourself and in this drawing, you look about eighty years old!'

I looked at my picture.[19]

I can't deny that he had a point.

'What's with all the wrinkles?' He picked my picture up by its corners and held it out in front of him for a closer inspection. I sighed and waited. 'And maybe those devil horns are a bit much too,' he finally added. 'Why don't you have another go and concentrate properly this time?'

But I couldn't be bothered to concentrate. And I couldn't be bothered to draw my own stupid Cornish pasty face so I just sat there in a big grizzly sulk and ignored everyone until it was lunchtime and then I got up and walked straight out of the school grounds because I didn't want to be there any longer.

Instead of turning right down Church Road and towards

---

[19] This is a quick approximation of what my *avant-garde* portrait looked like. The original piece of artwork is probably in a landfill site by now.

my house, I kept on walking down Merthyr Road and through the centre of Whitchurch village. Elvis Presley, a local celebrity who sleeps on a public bench and drinks more alcohol than is good for him, was dancing around on the opposite pavement and singing 'Jailhouse Rock' through a traffic cone. I wasn't in the mood to listen to him. Pulling my MP3 player out of my pocket, I shoved my earplugs into place and pressed the PLAY button. There was a second's delay and then an unmistakable clanking sound of feedback and percussion wrapped itself all around me and blocked Elvis Presley out of my life. Feeling relieved, I adjusted the volume so that no noise from the real world had any chance of getting through, and allowed Jimi Hendrix free rein to totally batter my ears. The freaky feedback noises faded away and Jimi's guitar burst its way into my head. Across the road, Elvis was now singing silently into his traffic cone. On my side of the street, people stood outside the shops and chatted with their volumes turned down. I smiled triumphantly and kept on walking – my footsteps in time to the music. I think I even had a bit of a swagger in my step. All of a sudden, I felt really good. I felt fantastic. I was swaggering along down Merthyr Road just as if I was in my very own MTV video and Jimi's song was ALL ABOUT ME.

And then it hit me.

The song I was listening to was called, 'Are You Experienced?'

Jimi, in his sexy but mocking voice, was asking me a question.

A very personal question.

And even though I'd listened to this song a thousand times before, it was only right there, at midday, in the middle of Whitchurch, that I suddenly understood exactly what he was driving at.

I stood stock still on the pavement. Jimi's weird guitar noises continued to blast my eardrums into a messy pulp. Instead of feeling fantastic, I suddenly felt a bit sick and dizzy. From out of nowhere, freaky visions popped into my head. There was Gareth in his pants and Goose with a colossal love bite on her neck and Dilys cracking sexy jokes and Neil Adam dating every single woman in Cardiff and Samantha Morgan and Lee Fogel in a disgusting pashy smoochy clinch. It was horrible.[20]

And it was also at that precise moment that I realized that EVERYONE in the whole of Cardiff is experienced except for me. I pulled the earplugs out of my ears and let them dangle down the front of my jumper. And then, before I even had a chance to stop and think about what I was doing, I took a great big deep breath and shouted,

'No, Jimi. I am NOT experienced. In fact, I'm a total virgin!'

All around, people stopped their conversations to turn and stare at me. I can't be sure that the cars didn't all screech to a skidding halt as well. It's actually even possible that the

---

[20] Except for the bit about Gareth in his pants.

world stopped spinning on its axis for a second. But then a man with a big belly, grey hair and fuzzy sideburns turned towards me as he pushed his way into the Spin Dizzy record shop and winked. He was braving the cold in a short-sleeved Cardiff City football shirt and had a matching Bluebirds tattoo on his big hairy arm. Grinning, he said, 'Anything *I* can help you out with, love?' And then he laughed like a leery person.

'Urrgghhh! Shut up!' I said. And then I turned and walked as fast as I could back up Merthyr Road and on towards my house.

And that's where I've been ever since. I haven't set foot outside the front door. I haven't dared to in case I lose my head and behave like a tragic desperado again. Yesterday, I told my mum I'd had to come home with a headache, and this morning I told her it hadn't gone away so she's let me stay off school. And I've just been typing all this up into my Emotion Notepad Document and having a very long hard think about stuff.

And what I've decided is this. It's about time I had some experience. Just like that nosy woman on the bus said, life passes by at the same speed that you can click your fingers. So there's no point messing about. It's time for me to wake up to reality and the reality is that I am a woman with a womanly urge. And I need to take action.

So I'm going to speak to Gareth tomorrow.

a shOrt DlsCusslON Of the DlfflCuLtles whlCh CaN arlse frOm BelNG NOt Qulte the MIDDLe ChlLD Of twO aND a haLf ChlLDreN

In science, I've been learning about a very boring thing called the periodic table. Basically, it's just a chart full of little boxes and in each little box is a symbol which represents a chemical element. In my opinion it's a colossally tedious diagram which is not worth looking at but my double science teacher, Mr Thomas, reckons that it's the most amazing feat of graphic design which has ever been undertaken. He says it's even more brilliant than the London Underground map. Personally, I don't think that the Underground map is any great shakes either. Mr Thomas loves the periodic table so much that he probably has it printed on his duvet cover and it wouldn't surprise me in the slightest to learn that he has the pillowcases to match. Anyway, he made us copy this boring chart into our boring exercise books and when we'd finished, he collected our books in to be marked. When I got mine back, he'd written all over my page in boring red pen because I'd got some of the boring boxes in the wrong boring order. I was a bit annoyed because I'd spent a lot of time colouring in that chart so that it looked nice. I said to him, 'At the end of the day, does anyone really care if I muddle up a couple of random elements like Scandium and Snoozium? In the great big scheme of things, does it *actually* matter?'

Mr Thomas folded his arms in a blatantly unfriendly manner and said, 'Yes, Lottie, in the great big scheme of things, it does matter, *actually*. It matters very much.'

'Why?' I said.

'Because,' said Mr Thomas, arching one eyebrow in a way that didn't make him look like James Bond, 'the periodic table has been brilliantly arranged so that each element is listed according to its atomic number and just by looking at the table we can also identify which family an element belongs to.' He unfolded his arms and tapped my drawing of the periodic table with his index finger. I stifled a yawn and tried to look vaguely interested. 'Each and every element,' he continued, 'was carefully and methodically placed for a reason. When the great Russian scientist Dmitri Mendeleev first came up with the design, he even left some gaps just so that any chemical elements which hadn't yet been discovered would have a place to slot in comfortably without upsetting the entire apple cart. The scientific world does not need *you* to come along and mess up the order of things, thank you very much. So make the changes that I've asked you to do and be more careful next time.'

Mr Thomas needs to lighten up.

But what this lesson did teach me is that there are times when it's crucial to have a fixed position in the great big scheme of things.

And I reckon that's part of the reason why I find life heavy going at times. I'm just like an undiscovered chemical element. I'm not exactly sure what my position is.

Until I was ten, I was perfectly clear about my position in the world. I was the very final box in my family's periodic table. I was the baby. Being the baby of the family has its drawbacks. It means that you have to wear your older sister's crappy hand-me-downs and it means that you get ordered up to bed while everyone else stays up watching the programmes with the swear words in them, and it means that all the teachers say annoying stuff like, 'Just try and do your best and don't worry if you're not as good as Ruthie.' But it has its upsides too. When you're the baby of the family, you tend to get a little bit spoilt by everyone. And sometimes, you get off scot-free for doing wrong stuff just because you're the youngest and you apparently don't understand. And if you ever have a fight with your sister, it's always *her* who gets into the most trouble even if you started it and you were beating her to a messy pulp. So, for me, being the baby had its ups and downs but at least I knew where I stood.

And then Caradoc came along and that confused everything. Now don't get me wrong, I'm not annoyed about Caradoc being born or anything horrible like that. I love him very much. But he does make life more complicated. It's not his fault. It's just the way things are.

Complicated.

You see, from the moment Caradoc was born I went from being a youngest child to being a middle child. My position in the periodic table shifted. But only for my dad. For my mum, I stayed right where I was in the final box on the chart. The baby of the family.

But how can I comfortably be the baby of the family when I have a brother who is ten years younger than me?

And even then, Caradoc's not my whole brother, he's my half-brother and, though I love him to bits, he doesn't actually feel like a real brother because I hardly ever see him. Every summer holiday, I go up to Wrexham and stay with my dad and Sally for a bit, and usually I visit during the Christmas holidays as well. But I don't go up very much more than that because Wrexham is about as far away from Cardiff as you can possibly go without leaving Wales. And then, very occasionally, my dad will bring him down to South Wales for a flying visit. But that's not very often. So really, if I'm completely honest, Caradoc feels more like a distant cousin. And while my sister Ruthie will ALWAYS know, without any shadow of doubt, that she is the eldest, I'm not totally sure where I stand any more.

Which does my head in sometimes.

And I think that this might be the reason why I get on everyone's nerves. I just float about between Cardiff and Wrexham not feeling exactly sure of who I am or how I'm meant to behave and now and again I get it all wrong. Sometimes I behave like the youngest when I'm not supposed to act like the youngest, and sometimes I just get irritated with Ruthie because her life is so flipping uncomplicated.

And it's when I get irritated that I'm most likely to do something or say something which will upset the apple cart and land me in a whole heap of trouble.

So it's mostly me that causes all the trouble and stress in my house. Even during the holidays when Ruthie is at home. Ruthie is a saint. She reads books and collects pottery and offers to cook for my mum and knows how the washing machine works. In fact, she's a perfect example of just how stable and grounded a person can be when they know their position in the world. Ruthie hardly *ever* gets into trouble.

Which is why I'm so excited about the fact that my mum is completely freaking out on Ruthie at this precise moment.

Earlier this evening, as planned, Ruthie turned up at our house with her friend, Michelle. Except that it turns out that Michelle is not some boring girl she's studying with at all. *He* is actually a French exchange student called Michel and 'studying' seems to be the last thing on their minds. Michel has floppy dark hair and wears his jumper tucked into corduroy trousers which are slightly too short for him. And every time he thinks that me and mum aren't looking, he pushes Ruthie's hair back from her face and puts his tongue in her ear.

QUICK!

IN CASE OF ILLNESS

When they arrived, my mum pulled Ruthie into the kitchen and said, 'You could have told me you were bringing a *man*! I'll have to make up a camp bed for him in the living room now.'

Ruthie said, 'Oh, don't worry. He can stay in my room.'

My mum hissed, 'He most certainly CAN NOT!'

And then I said, 'Mum, are we still having that girly night in tomorrow because I've changed my mind and I REALLY FANCY the idea now.'

My mum looked my way with a face which would frighten a Rottweiler, but instead of having a go at me, she turned to Ruthie and said, 'You can be SOOOO inconsiderate sometimes, young lady.'

Ruthie just said, 'So I'm seeing a gorgeous Frenchman and I've brought him home for the weekend. So what?' And then she turned to me and said, 'And you can shut up, Fart Face.'

Now I come to think about it, Ruthie *isn't* a saint. But,

if anything, that makes me like her slightly more. And it's about time she took some of the heat for a change.

I said, 'Oh shut up, Fish Breath,' and then I came up here to my bedroom to get away from her.

In my Oscar Wilde book, there is a line which says,

> *'Children begin by loving their parents; as they grow older they judge them; sometimes they forgive them.'*

Oscar Wilde may be boring but there's no denying the fact that he's extremely wise. I think that my parents have to accept that it's partly their fault that I'm difficult because they are the ones responsible for making me not quite the middle child of two and a half children.

I've got no idea what Ruthie's excuse is.

But aCtuaLLY there are NO eXCuses

I don't think that Blake fully understands the enormity of the task he's set me. Writing this Emotion Notepad is eating up hours and hours of my life and I'm still only skimming the surface of my cosmic complexities. This weekend perfectly illustrates my problem. It's not even over yet and already I've got too much to write about. Since Ruthie and Monsieur Loverman arrived on Friday, I've experienced a whole series of emotional shock waves which have threatened to hurl me off balance as I surf my way back to inner calm and mental well-being. My head is so full of discombobulating[21] experiences that now I've fired up my computer and sat down to write I don't know which discombobulating shock wave to talk about first. My hair is screaming out at me to start with all the putrid details of its tragic transformation, but my heart says I should begin by discussing the shocking discovery I made in Ruthie's toilet bag. But then again, perhaps I should talk about how, last night, I tried to get it on with Gareth and only ended up turning him off completely. Or maybe I should start with the dodgy wobble I had in the hair salon?

Mr Wood always advises us to begin at the beginning so I'll start with the salon.

Yesterday was my second Saturday of employment at

---

[21] This is my FAVOURITE word ever. It means disturbing. Goose likes this word as well but only because she copied me.

The Jean Genie and it was also nearly my last. Just like the week before, I arrived at the salon over an hour early but this time it was on purpose because I couldn't stand being at home a single second longer than I needed to be. The thought of being under the same roof as a couple of loved-up archaeology students was too hideous to contemplate. I've been opening windows whenever I can but I'm convinced that the air in our house is still swarming with their sex hormones. To be honest, it makes me feel a bit queasy just thinking about it.

When Jean arrived, she said, 'Early again, Lottie? There's nothing quite like being an early bird, is there?'

'I know, it's brilliant,' I said. 'I always catch the worm.' To be honest, I was just making small talk.

Jean unlocked the shop and said, 'You had such a good day last week, Lottie, that I'm going to give you an extra responsibility. I'm going to let you do some hair washing.'

'Brilliant,' I said. 'I'm good at hair washing.'

'Ah,' said Jean, 'but have you ever washed anyone else's hair? It's a very particular and specialized skill.'

'No,' I said, 'but I was watching Neil very closely last week and I think I spotted all the important stuff.' I counted off my observations, one by one, on my fingers. 'White towels are for regular use and navy towels are for clients who are having a colour application. Press their heads a bit after you've rinsed all the shampoo out and remember to ask them about their holidays.'

Jean smiled. 'Not bad, Lottie, not bad at all, but you've

missed a couple of absolute hairdressing essentials. *Don't forget* to ask them if the temperature of the water is OK and *don't forget* to ask them if they have anything nice planned for the weekend. Can you manage that?'

'Er, I think so,' I said. Jean Stingecombe is very nice but I do feel that she occasionally underestimates my abilities.

Just then, Neil and Dilys came through the door together. Neil was wearing a shiny plastic leopard-print raincoat and Dilys was wearing a knitted poncho. The pair of them looked quite avant-garde for this part of Cardiff.

Dilys said, 'Ooooh, I was walking to work when this handsome young stranger pulled up in his car and offered me a lift.' She winked at Neil. 'Nice to know I can still stop the traffic at my age.'

Neil took off his leopard-print raincoat and winked back at her. 'There's always a place for your booty in my broom-broom, Dil,' he said, and then he looked at me and said, 'All right, gorgeous?'

Instead of replying with anything cool, I just squeaked something stupid that sounded like, 'Yip,' and then when I'd recovered a bit, I said, 'I didn't know you had wheels, Neil.'

Neil twirled his car keys around his index finger and said, 'Just passed my test and I got myself a hot red Fiat Panda passion wagon to celebrate.'

'Oooh, I bet the girls love it, don't they, Neily?' added Dilys.

Neil ignored Dilys and looked me right in the eye.

'There's a lot you don't know about me, Lottie Biggs. In fact, there's a lot that *the entire world* doesn't know about Neil Adam. I am a Welsh enigma.'

'Now now, Neily,' said Jean, who was showing the first customer of the day into a chair by the basins. 'I've told you before, leave Lottie alone and stop flirting. You know she's unavailable.'

'That's what I like about her,' said Neil with a big grin.

Jean put a protective arm around my shoulder and said, 'Ignore him, Lottie. He thinks he's a player. Now can you give Mrs John a shampoo, please?' And then she gave me a meaningful look and added, 'And remember what we talked about earlier.'

I nodded and went off to the cupboard to get a couple of white towels for Mrs John's hair. Mrs John is about eighty and her hair is cotton-wool white. When I returned, I placed one towel around Mrs John's shoulders and put the other on a nearby chair, ready to be twisted into a turban on Mrs John's head when I'd finished. Then I helped Mrs John to lean backwards into the sink and began spraying her hair with the sprinkler.

'Is the water all right for you?' I asked.

'Yes dear, it's lovely,' replied Mrs John.

'Are you going anywhere nice for your holidays?' I asked.

'No dear,' replied Mrs John.

'Did you do anything nice last night?' I asked.

'No dear,' replied Mrs John.

'You doing anything nice tonight?' I asked.

'No dear,' replied Mrs John.

'You doing anything nice tomorrow night?' I asked.

'No dear,' replied Mrs John.

'You doing anything nice Monday night?' I asked.

Mrs John didn't respond. I was about to put my sprinkler aside and check that she was still breathing when she suddenly said, 'Well, I don't know, dear. It's a toss-up, see, between going pole dancing down Cardiff Bay or lap dancing in town. What do you think I should do?'

'Urgghh! Shut up!' I said.

From the other side of the salon, Jean Stingecombe rushed over and said, 'LOTTIE, I'D LIKE A WORD WITH YOU UPSTAIRS, PLEASE.' And then, to Mrs John, she gave a big apologetic smile and said, 'Sorry, Blodwyn. Lottie's a *gorgeous* girl but she's a little bit highly strung.'

'No I'm not,' I said.

'UPSTAIRS, PLEASE,' barked Jean Stingecombe. And then in a normal voice, she added, 'Neily, look after Mrs John for me, will you, my lovely?'

When we were upstairs in the staffroom, Jean said, 'You *can't* go telling the clients to shut up, Lottie. What's got into you?'

I didn't really know what the answer to this question was so I just kept my mouth shut. My brain was buzzing about like a bumblebee gone bananas though.

'Lottie,' said Jean. 'Can you explain to me why I just

heard you telling lovely Mrs John to shut up?'

I closed my eyes for a moment and pressed my hands against my head as if I was trying to stop it from falling off. Then I counted silently to ten, took a deep calming breath and tried to picture myself as a cosmic surfer on a peaceful intergalactic wave. By the time I'd finished doing all of this, I felt a lot more steady and in control.

Then I said, 'She was being rude and I was just trying to be nice to her and make conversation like you said and she started talking about sexy dancing and stuff and I think she was just deliberately trying to wind me up and embarrass me and I'm getting fed up with it to be honest because everyone is always going on about sex in this place and it does my head in because Neil is always making sexy comments and so is Dilys and it's just sex sex sex all the time and now Mrs John is at it as well and it gets on my nerves because everybody knows that the people who go on about it all the time are probably not getting any action anyway!'

By the time I'd finished, I was completely out of breath.

Jean Stingecombe was staring at me with a smile frozen on her face. She had suddenly gone as still as a sleepy chinchilla.

I put my knuckles into my mouth and bit them. Then I said, 'And I'm not highly strung either.'

'Noooo,' said Jean very slowly.

Something about the tone of her voice gave me the impression that she didn't believe me so I added, 'No, actually, I'm not.'

Jean Stingecombe continued to look at me as if she didn't believe me. I chewed my knuckles some more and sighed noisily. Finally, I said, 'Look, Mrs Stingecombe, I've got one or two issues that I'm having to deal with at the moment. I don't really want to talk about it. But it's got nothing to do with being highly strung.'

'You can call me Jean,' replied Jean Stingecombe immediately. Her frozen smile turned into a thoughtful frown. After what seemed like ages, she said, 'You're absolutely right. Dilys and Neil do overstep the mark sometimes. I'll have a word with them and tell them to tone it down a bit. I know they're only messing around but that kind of talk isn't appropriate in the workplace.' Then she said, 'But that's still no excuse for telling lovely Mrs John to shut up, is it, Lottie?'

'I'm not sure,' I said. I was actually being very honest. The entire conversation was starting to spin my head out.

Jean walked over to the scaly kettle which lives on the worktop and filled it up at the sink. 'What I mean,' she said, turning to talk to me, 'is that *your* . . .' She paused for a second as if she were searching for the best words. '. . . your *issues* may go a little way to explaining *why* you got upset with Mrs John but it doesn't mean that it was *OK* to be rude to her. *Your* . . .' She paused again.

I sank down into a chair and put my head in my hands. I could tell that Jean was still frantically scanning her personal inner thesaurus. The silence was awful. I decided to help her out. 'Mental disturbance of a reasonably significant nature,' I mumbled, and then I looked up because I wanted to catch the reaction on Jean's face.

It didn't even flicker. '. . .Your mental disturbance is not like the joker in a deck of cards. You can't just get it out and wave it in the air as an excuse any time you break the rules a little bit.'

'I never said it *was* an excuse,' I answered, feeling slightly cross.

'But *you're* the one who brought the subject up,' said Jean Stingecombe with a small smile. And then she pushed a mug of tea into my hands. 'So where are we gonna go from here?' she asked.

I looked at the mug of tea and thought hard about my conversations with Blake.

Finally, I mumbled, 'I'll say sorry to Mrs John and I won't tell anyone else to shut up.'

'That's my lovely girl,' said Jean with a bigger smile. 'Now you finish your tea and come out when you're ready. It's *always* difficult being the new person at work — but don't you worry, I'll sort out Neil and Dilys.' And then she reached out and patted me softly on my shoulder and went back down to the salon.

I sat still in my chair and clutched my mug of tea. For some reason, I was finding it quite hard not to cry.

Jean Stingecombe is OK, you know. And to be fair to her, she can be as deep as Oscar Wilde when she wants to be. I'm not surprised that she's Gareth's mum.

hair MutiLatiON 1

As if by magic, Gareth appeared in the salon a few seconds before my lunch break. He was wearing his red Wales rugby shirt and a chunky grey scarf because it was turning cold. He looked fairly SEXADELIC, if I'm honest. I can't tell you how pleased I was to see him. I don't think that Noah could have been any more pleased when he spotted dry land. 'I'm treating you to whatever you fancy at the Dragon Coffee House,' Gareth said. 'I reckon it must be hard work being in here all day with my mum and Dilys.'

Jean laughed and gave Gareth a clip round the ear. Not hard, just friendly. Dilys said, 'Oooh, Jean, he's a saucy one, is your Razzy-Gazzy. Who'd have thought that your sweet baby boy would grow up to become such a cheeky great hunk of chunk?'

Gareth's face turned the same colour as his top. I said, 'Don't forget I've got Neil here as well, Gaz.'

Neil looked over from where he was blow-drying Mr Pugsley's rock-a-billy quiff, and winked.

Gareth scowled, put his hand on my shoulder and practically shoved me out of the door.

Over at the Dragon Coffee House, I ordered a double choco-mochaccino (with extra cream and chocolate flakes) and a large plate of chips with ketchup. Gareth ordered a pint of coke, two Dragon burgers with extra cheese, a side order of onion rings and a sausage roll. 'If you don't mind,

I'll just share your chips, Lottie,' he said. 'Coach Jenkins reckons I need to keep myself nice and solid for the field of play but there's no point overdoing it and eating like a pig, is there?'

If anyone else had ordered all of that and then said this, I'd have thought they were madder than I am but Gareth has a very impressive physical frame and it requires a lot of fuel. Dilys is right about him. He is a hunk of chunk.

Gareth reached into the pocket of his jeans and said, 'Oh yeah, I've got something for you.' On the table he placed two cinema tickets. '*Shark Mutilation 3*. Tonight. You and me at the Ponty-Carlo Picture House.' He gave me a shy grin. 'I can take a hint, Lottie, but next time, if you wanna go and see a film, just ask me.'

'Thanks, Gareth,' I said. 'That's brilliant.' And then I added, 'Um, I don't suppose I could come and have lunch round at your place tomorrow, could I?'

Gareth pulled a horrified face. 'You don't wanna come round my house! My mum and dad will behave all weird and get my baby photos out.'

I laughed. 'When you put it like that, it does sound terrible, but I sort of told my mum that I was having lunch round yours tomorrow.'

Gareth looked at me as if I'd just said, 'Isn't double science amazing?'

'It was to get me out of doing something even worse,' I added.

'Oh, OK then.' Gareth seemed less confused. 'I'll have

a word with my mum. She won't mind. She thinks you're nice.' And then he added with a sly grin, 'And Dilys thinks you're a sweet honey bunny.'

I squeezed his knee under the table and said, 'Oh yeah? And what does Neil Adam think?'

Gareth pushed my hand away and said crossly, 'I don't care what that scatty womanizer thinks.'

I reached into Gareth's lap and took hold of his hand. We sat there quietly in the middle of the busy cafe with our hands joined under the table. Suddenly, my heart was beating like the bass line in a Jimi Hendrix record. I cleared my throat and said, 'Actually, Gareth, there's something else I wanted to ask you.'

Gareth rolled his eyes and said, 'Oh, what now? I've already said you can come and meet my embarrassing family tomorrow.'

'No, it's not that,' I said. 'It's just that we've been going out for quite a while now and . . .'

Gareth looked appalled. 'You're not going to dump me, are you? Not here. Not now. Not like this. You've just invited yourself round my house! I thought you and me were getting on OK!'

'No, it's nothing like that,' I said really quickly. 'In fact, it's the opposite. I think we get on so well that I think we should . . .' I paused. I was starting to feel a bit hot and embarrassed.

'What?' said Gareth.

'Well, maybe, you know . . .'

'One double choco-mochaccino with extra cream and chocolate flakes,' said a voice at my shoulder, causing me to jump. 'One pint of cola. One large plate of chips with ketchup. Two Dragon burgers and one sausage roll.' The waitress plonked the food down in front of us.

'I ordered onion rings as well,' said Gareth anxiously.

'They're on their way,' replied the waitress and then disappeared again.

Gareth picked up one of his burgers and took a huge bite out of it. 'What were you saying, Biggsy?

I stirred my choco-mochaccino nervously. I was very close to abandoning the subject, if I'm honest. But then I reminded myself that I am sexually frustrated and that piece of personal information was so humiliating that I decided to try again.

'Well, we like each other, don't we?' I said.

'Yes,' said Gareth, picking up his pint of cola.

'So, maybe we should . . .'

'One side order of onion rings,' said the waitress and dumped them down on the table.

'Ta,' said Gareth, putting a whole one straight into his mouth.

I took a deep breath. 'I just think that as we're approaching our late teens, we—'

'Er . . . we're fifteen,' said Gareth.

'Yeah, well, we're both in our mid to late teens and I think that perhaps we should—'

Just then Goose and Spud walked through the door,

causing me to shut up abruptly. They took seats at the only empty table, which just happened to be right next to ours. Spud called out, 'Stingey! My main man! What's going down?'

Gareth said, 'Spudley! Bruv! How's it hanging?'

Spud said, 'Stingey! You legend! What's the word on the street?'

Gareth said, 'Spudley! I am the walrus! And you knows it!'

Goose looked at me politely and said, 'Hi.'

And I said, 'Hi,' back.

Then Gareth turned back to me and said, 'Sorry, Lottie, what was you on about before?'

And this time I did abandon the subject. 'I was thinking that perhaps we should split this bill,' I said. 'Seems only fair, really.'

Gareth gave me one of his huge and lovely smiles. 'You know what, Biggsy? Some of the suggestions you come up with are totally flipping amazing.' And then he winked at me and I have to admit that it was a much nicer wink than Neil Adam could ever manage.

At half past four, just as I was polishing the last mirror, Jean Stingecombe locked the door of the salon and hung the *Closed* sign in the window. I put down my bottle of vinegar and scrunched-up ball of newspaper and said, 'More staff development, is it?'

'Certainly is, Lottie,' said Jean. 'It's a tight ship we've got here. Staff development is crucial to ensure we don't get left behind in the competitive cut and thrust of the Cardiff hair fashion industry. Go and wash that vinegar off your hands and we'll make a start.'

As I walked up to the staffroom, I heard Dilys say, 'Ooh, whose hair are we developing today, Jee? Neil's or Lottie's?'

'I don't mind volunteering,' I heard Neil say. 'I've had this style for a whole week now. I could probably do with a change. Maybe something shorter . . . more brushed forward. Quite sharp around my temples. I think it's called a Caesar. Yeah, I'm sure it is. You can give me a Caesar if you like.'

Alone in the staffroom, I ran my hands under the tap, not really caring whether I was removing all the newsprint and the smell of vinegar. My mind was elsewhere. Since the episode with Mrs John, the day had been OK but the memory of my pole-dancing-related outburst was still a bit raw. I knew I'd shown myself up and I wanted to put things right. More than anything, I wanted to show Jean that I wasn't highly strung. Drying my hands quickly on my culottes, I took a deep breath and returned to the salon. Neil was already taking up his position in the demonstration chair.

'It's all right, Neil,' I said. 'You did it last week. It's my turn.'

Neil shrugged and stood up.

Dilys said, 'Oooh, what are we going to do with Lottie's hair, Jee? A shaggy perm?'

Jean Stingecombe looked a little doubtful. 'Are you absolutely sure you want to do this, Lottie?' she said. 'Neil has already offered and it does require a certain spirit of adventure to volunteer for a restyle.'

I sat down in the demonstration chair. 'I've got a spirit of adventure,' I said, suddenly feeling quite reckless. 'Do whatever you like.' And then I added, 'But not a shaggy perm, though.'

Jean smiled. 'OK then. I won't do anything too drastic this time and then, if you like, we could do something a bit more radical another day.'

And then she began snipping and combing and curling my hair, and while she did all this, she sang *'Yoo-hoo make me feeeeel, yoo-hoo make me feeeeel, yoo-hoo make me feeeeeeeel like an act-u-al wo-man,'* along to the song which was coming out of the salon's speakers and was, in fact, almost always coming out of the salon's speakers.

And when she'd finished, I looked like this:

I sat very still in the demonstration chair and looked at myself in the mirror.

'What do you think?' said Jean.

I swallowed hard and counted to twenty in my head. My forehead had gone very sweaty. Finally, I said, 'Umm, I think it makes me look quite a lot older.'

It did as well. I looked at least sixty.

Dilys said, 'Oooh Lottie, you look just like a young Queen Elizabeth.'

I almost screamed, 'No, I don't. I look just like an *old* Queen Elizabeth!' But I didn't. Because I'm not highly strung.

Jean beamed and said, 'Didn't I say I make my clients look like royalty? What do you think, Neily?'

Neil growled at me and said, 'Hold me back, you cheeky regal temptress.'

Jean said, 'Less of that kind of talk in here please, Neil. It's not appropriate for the workplace – and don't let my Gazzy hear you talking like that. Now, Lottie, it's a very classic style I've given you. Very chic and very feminine. But if it's not quite to your liking, you only need to give it a couple of washes and all those ridges and curls will soon disappear.'

I swallowed again and said, 'Thanks, Jean. I like it. I do. It's nice.'

Jean looked chuffed to bits.

Before my mind had time to change direction, I collected my bag from the staffroom and waved goodbye to everyone.

They waved back and I left the salon without giving a single hint of the battle which had just taken place within me. Even writing about it now makes me feel quite proud. Because, as I'd sat rigid in that chair and contemplated the full horror of my queenly hairdo, I'd *almost* lost it. A tidal wave had threatened my balance. I'd felt the surfboard wobble perilously beneath me and I'd been a single nanosecond away from pitching head first into the deadly whirlpools of chaos.

But I hadn't. I'd seen that tidal wave coming and surfed right over the top of it.

shark MutILatION 3

The Ponty-Carlo Picture House has been in Whitchurch for as long as I can remember. In fact, it's been in Whitchurch for as long as my mum can remember too. There is only one screen – which is framed by gigantic dirty orange curtains – and the rows of seats are so tightly packed together that it's quite normal to come out after the film with bumps and bruises on your knees. It's also fairly common to come out with chewing gum stuck to the backside of your trousers. On rainy days, the Ponty-Carlo smells of two hundred pairs of wet trainers. On dry days, it just smells of feet. Sometimes the man who works in the projector room falls asleep and lets the film slip upwards so that all the actors' and actresses' heads are missing and the bottom half of the screen is just a blinding band of white light. When this happens, we all stamp our feet on the floor and hammer on the back of the chair in front of us and shout and scream until the projector man wakes up and puts it right again. All my life, Pat Mumble has sold us choc ices there. Pat Mumble sold choc ices to my mum when she was a girl too. We know her name is Pat because it says so on her name badge. She's earned the surname Mumble because her mouth is always full of sweets whenever she speaks to us and all we can ever hear is, 'Mumble mumble mumble.' It's fair to say that the Ponty-Carlo is not the most glamorous cinema in Cardiff but everybody loves it because it's cheap. This is where Gareth took me to see *Shark Mutilation 3* and this is where I tried, once more, to raise the subject of *it*.

For once, it didn't take me long to get ready. My queenly hairdo hadn't left me with many options. I whacked on some lipstick, chucked on some mascara, smudged on a bit of glittery eye shadow and changed into my favourite flowery jumper dress, hot pants and stripy tights. Then, knowing that I had a full-blown hair crisis on my hands and needing to deal with the problem sensibly and efficiently, I added my final accessory.

It wasn't ideal and the hat, which had once belonged to my dad, was a bit too big but it was the only one I could find. And it was still better than going out looking like my nan.

When I went downstairs, my mum said, 'Ooh, very glamorous!'

I said, 'Shut up. You're beginning to sound like Dilys at work.'

My mum said, 'Will you stop telling people to shut up! It's so rude.'

Ruthie, who was sitting on the sofa practically in Michel's lap, whistled and said, 'Wow! Doesn't my little brother look cute!'

Ruthie can be all right sometimes – when she's asleep or in Aberystwyth – but mostly, she's just a pathetic fish.

Michel said, 'You English girls have such a strange sense of fashion.'

'WE'RE NOT ENGLISH,' said me, Ruthie and my mum all at once. 'WE'RE WELSH!'

Michel looked deeply confused and a little bit alarmed. He didn't say anything after that.

Just then the doorbell rang and I went to answer it. It was Gareth. He had changed into his bright yellow Welsh away shirt which he was wearing with his chunky grey scarf and jeans. He looked absolutely SEXALICIOUS!

When he saw me he said, 'Wow, Lottie! Cool bobble hat! Did my mum mess up your hair?'

This is why I like him so much. Unlike everyone else in the world, me and Gareth Stingecombe are on completely the same wavelength.

After a short walk in the rain, we arrived at the Ponty-Carlo. There was already a large queue outside. Plainly, the people of Cardiff like to see heads popping during a shark attack. Gareth waved his tickets proudly and said, 'Prepurchased especially for the babe in the bobble hat. No need to queue. We can just go straight in and choose the best seats.'

I held Gareth's hand and walked with him into the glittery entrance foyer. As we jumped the queue, I heard someone shout, 'Look at Potty Lottie! She's got a tea cosy on her head!'

I turned round and saw Lee Fogel sneering at me. He was with Samantha Morgan. I was just about to yell back at him when I noticed that Samantha had tugged on Lee's arm and was saying something into his ear. She looked quite cross. I think they were arguing again. Gareth put his arm around me and said, 'Ignore him, Lottie. Lee Fogel has got biscuits inside his head instead of brains.'

This is another reason why I like Gareth so much.

Inside the foyer, Pat Mumble said, 'Mumble mumble mumble,' and ripped our tickets in two. Gareth bought a giant bucket of toffee popcorn and an extra large cola for each of us and one small bag of chocolate peanuts to share. 'I'll get you a choc ice in the interval,' he said. 'But it's good to have something to keep us going until then.'

This reminds me of another thing I like about the Ponty-Carlo. It's the only cinema I've ever been to which has an interval. First it shows some rubbish local adverts, then it shows a short film which always makes no sense and looks as if it's been filmed using a mobile phone and some actors from a local drama club, and then, after an interval where we all queue up to buy a choc ice from Pat Mumble, we get to see 'the main feature'.

'Did Coach Jenkins tell you that you need to eat a lot of sugary stuff?' I said to Gareth as I took hold of my bucket of popcorn, which just happened to be about the same size as my entire head.

Gareth looked impressed. 'Yeah, he did actually. How did you know that?'

'Just a hunch,' I said.

Once inside the cinema, I saw that we were nearly the first to take our seats. Gareth was about to head straight for the front row, when I pulled him back by the arm. He turned round with a look of surprise. 'Quick,' he said. 'We should nab a couple of seats right down the front before everyone else comes in. I love it in the front row. It's immense. Everything looks so huge that it makes your head spin.'

'Yes, but it's not very . . .' I hesitated.

'Not very what?' asked Gareth, licking cola off the lid of his drink container.

'Romantic,' I said.

'Oh, right!' Gareth stopped licking the lid of his drink and grinned. 'Seats at the very back then, is it?'

Taking control because I could see that I blatantly needed to, I grabbed Gareth's hand and led him to the furthest and most private corner of the cinema. We were right on the very back row. The row which everyone knows is always reserved exclusively for lovers. After a quick check for chewing gum, we settled down into our seats. People were now streaming into the cinema and the lights had already gone down. The shabby orange curtains jerked backwards and an advertisement for a Cardiff carpet cleaning company began to play on the screen. Gareth had his knees wedged up tightly against the seat in front. He was wearing his smartest pair of jeans. I sat up and stared ahead of me and watched the ad. Different people in different front rooms were spilling cups of tea and glasses of wine on to their different carpets. All these spillages were taking place to a pumping backing track of the Britney Spears hit, *Oops! . . . I Did It Again*. I closed my eyes for a moment and then looked back down at Gareth's jeans. As much as I tried to stare through them, it was impossible to know which boxer shorts he had on underneath. Taking hold of his hand, I leaned into his shoulder and said quietly, 'Gareth, there's something I want to talk to you about before the film starts.'

'Cool. Fire away, I'm listening,' said Gareth, pushing a handful of popcorn into his mouth while his eyes remained keenly glued to the ad which was now trying to sell us car tyres.

'You and me,' I said in a low voice, 'we've been going out for quite a while now . . .'

Gareth stopped munching popcorn and looked at me horrified. 'You're not about to dump me again, are you?'

I frowned. 'I didn't dump you before, Gaz,' I said. 'How can I be dumping you *again* if I didn't dump you before? I don't know what you're on about.'

Gareth shrugged. 'Well, as long as we're clear that no dumping activity is about to take place.' He took another handful of popcorn. 'So what did you want to talk to me about?'

I hesitated, trying to think of how I should put it.

Gareth laughed and kissed my nose and said, 'You've forgotten, haven't you? Lottie has *forgottie* what she wants to talk about!'

'No I haven't,' I said and rubbed some popcorn crumbs off his face so that I could kiss him back. After paying attention to his nose, I moved downward and paid attention to his lips. They tasted all sugary and kissing them gave me a big fizzy sugar rush. Energized, I pulled my lips away from his and said in a weirdly husky voice, 'I think we should do the Grand Slam, Gaz.'

Gareth looked interested. In a voice which was blatantly brimming with excitement, he said, 'Well, Wales does have a very good record in the Six Nations, Lottie, so there's every possibility that we can pull off another Grand Slam. Every possibility. I, personally, am very optimistic about our chances.'

I sat back in my chair and frowned. Mostly me and Gareth *are* on the same wavelength but, admittedly, not always.

I decided to be direct. There was no point messing around any more. 'No, Gareth,' I said, my voice now a whisper. 'I think it's time that we had sex.'

Gareth coughed and a few pieces of popcorn flew out of

his mouth and plastered themselves on to the back of the chair in front. If Gareth wasn't so gorgeous and I wasn't feeling so erotically charged, I might have found that fairly disgusting.

When he'd finished coughing, Gareth shook his head as if he had water in his ears and whispered, 'Am I hearing straight? Did you just say that you wanna . . .' he paused, embarrassed, and then said, 'do *it*?'

I nodded at him in the dark. I had started to giggle. Sometimes, I find it absolutely impossible to have a grown-up conversation about a grown-up subject without giggling. It's a very annoying problem actually. In fact, I wouldn't be at all surprised if it's some sort of medical syndrome. It's like that time when I was twelve and my mum barged into my bedroom to do 'the period conversation'. She was carrying a maxi-pack of jumbo jammy rags and said, 'I think you and I need to have a little chat because it won't be very long before you have to use one of these things.' And I'd taken one look at those great big knicker-surfboards and started to giggle. But instead of doing the most helpful thing and giggling with me, my mum had gone bright red and got a bit cross and said, 'Maybe I got that wrong. Maybe you're not growing up as fast as I think you are.' And then she'd walked out of my room and left me sitting alone on my bed with the jammy rags, still giggling but feeling a bit pathetic at the same time.

And that was just how I felt in the cinema with Gareth. I was giggling about sex and hating myself for giggling about it all at the same time.

Gareth wasn't giggling. His eyes had gone very big and round and I could see the white bits gleaming at me in the dark. 'You're completely serious, aren't you?' he whispered.

'Yep,' I said and giggled like a silly wet fish.

Gareth whispered, 'No way! We can't! Not here. There isn't enough room. And anyway, there are too many people around. And it smells of pongy old trainers. It doesn't seem right.'

'I don't mean *right this second*,' I said. 'But somewhere else. Soon.'

'Oh!' Gareth gave a massive sigh of relief. I felt his whole body relax. 'You had me a bit worried for a moment. I thought you meant *in here*. Personally, I prefer a bit of space and privacy when I'm, you know . . . doing *it*.'

'Have you done *it* before?' I whispered in surprise.

Gareth put a piece of popcorn between his teeth and bit it. 'Well, no . . . not technically *the entire business*, but . . .' He paused and stared straight ahead. On the screen, there was now an advertisement for stairlifts.

'But what?' I whispered.

Gareth put his popcorn down into his lap and sighed noisily. 'But I know that I definitely *would like* a bit of space and privacy if I *was* doing it. Now can you just let me watch the stuff on the screen, please?' And then he pushed another huge handful of popcorn into his mouth and watched the advert for stairlifts very very intently.

Next to him, I sat in my seat and tried to do the same but I couldn't concentrate. It was impossible. It didn't matter whether I was watching old ladies go up the stairs in a stairlift or dog owners telling me how much their pets enjoyed *Taffy Pets Healthy Food Products*, all I could think about was the fact that Gareth Stingecombe's body was sitting right next to mine and I was deeply desirous of it.

Meanwhile, Gareth sat very quietly and ate his popcorn. When he'd finished it all, he whispered, 'Are you gonna eat yours or what?'

I shook my head. 'I'm not that hungry, Gaz. Only for you.'

Gareth frowned a bit in the dark. 'All right, babe. Be cool.' And then he said, 'Can I have your popcorn then?'

I handed my barely touched bucket of popcorn to him. The short film began. It was called *Comfort Eating* and it was about a man eating a Chinese takeaway inside a phone box. When he had finished eating all the prawn crackers and sweet and sour pork and egg fried rice, he ate all the packaging too. And then he tried to phone God but the phone was broken.

When it finished, the lights came up and Pat Mumble stood at the front of the cinema carrying her white tray filled with choc ices. Gareth stretched and got up from his seat. 'Do you wanna choc ice, Lottie?'

'No,' I said. 'And we've still got those chocolate peanuts, don't forget.'

'No we haven't. I ate them during that last film. Sure

you don't wanna choc ice? I'm having one. I can't go to the cinema and not have a choc ice. Don't seem right.' He stood up and walked down to the front where Pat Mumble was. I watched him while he queued and then I watched him as he walked back to his seat. A great big hunk of chunk carrying a choc ice.

Shark Mutilation 3 is the most unpleasant film I've ever seen. I rate it very poorly against any of the *Free Willy* offerings. I don't actually know why I even thought I might like to see it. It's probably because everyone at school has been going on and on about it for weeks. Basically, it's about a group of American teenagers who are on their way to Hawaii to attend a beauty pageant when their plane crashes and falls into the sea. Everyone else on the plane drowns instantly but they are left alive and clinging to the wreckage while a pack of sharks circles them, getting closer and closer. One by one they get chewed up and eaten, and just as each person is on the brink of death, the film goes all fuzzy and we get flashbacks of the most meaningful moments in their lives. I can't explain what happens in the end though because I never actually got to see it.

Gareth clearly hadn't been enjoying the film either. He'd eaten his choc ice without a word to me and had flinched whenever anybody's limb got ripped away from their body. I felt responsible. After all, it was my fault that we were here. In an effort to put things right, I decided to try to take his mind away from the horror on the screen. In the darkest and most private corner of the cinema, I put my hand on Gareth

Stingecombe's leg. Gareth placed his big hand on top of mine and stroked it. We sat like that for a while trying not to watch as one of the unlucky beautiful teenagers slipped off the plane wreckage and got eaten. After a few minutes, I wriggled my hand out from underneath Gareth's and slowly slid it higher up his leg. I felt his body stiffen. All around us were the sounds of shrieks and screams and crashing waves but I barely noticed them. Holding my breath, I let my hand travel a little further until it stopped on top of Gareth's personal regions. Gareth didn't move a muscle. I could hear him breathing in and out quite deeply though and his head had flopped forward. Without daring to turn my head a single millimetre, I used my fingertips to feel for Gareth's zip and slowly undid his fly. Gareth leaned forward a little in his seat and put one hand up to his mouth. I guessed that it was to try to stem the tide of passion which was making him want to shout out loud and declare his desire for me to everyone in the cinema.[22] Still, holding the rest of my body perfectly still, I slipped my fingers inside his jeans.

At exactly the same moment, the famous head-popping scene popped messily all over the screen. The audience all went,

'ARGGGGGG-HHHHHHHH!'

---

[22] On reflection, I now think I was wrong.

Gareth went,

'URRGGGGGGGG-
HHHHHHHHHH!'

And then he clapped his hand over his mouth, shot to his feet and rushed out through the emergency exit.

For ten minutes, I sat by myself, unsure of what to do. Finally, the light of a torch made its way towards me through the darkness and a voice whispered, 'Mumble mumble mumble Lottie?'

'Yes,' I said.

Pat Mumble said, 'Mumble mumble mumble Gareth mumble mumble mumble outside.'

'Oh,' I said. 'Thanks.'

I picked up my bag and followed Pat Mumble out of the cinema. When we reached the foyer, she pointed to the main entrance doors, rolled her eyes up to the ceiling and said, 'Mumble mumble mumble kids,' and then shuffled off back to the dark and screaming world of mutilation by sharks.

Outside, Gareth was squatting against the wall with his head in his hands. It was clear for anyone to see that he had been very badly sick all over the pavement. He looked up at me and said, 'Sorry.' Then he looked down at the ground again.

'It's OK,' I said and touched his shoulder. 'What's up?'

Gareth clutched his stomach miserably. 'I dunno, Lottie. I'm wondering if I ate too much. While that film was on, my belly started to feel a bit funny. And then there was all that gore and blood on the screen . . . and then you started prodding my nudger . . .' He rubbed his face against the sleeve of his rugby shirt. 'It just made me feel too weird. I needed to hurl.' He looked at me apologetically. 'Sorry.'

I bit my thumbnail and looked at him. I'll be honest, it doesn't make you feel fantastic when the person you really fancy tells you that they've just chucked up because you touched their personal regions. I pulled my bobble hat down tighter on to my head in the way that I've seen celebrities do in those celebrity stalker magazines. It made me feel slightly better. I could almost feel myself disappearing. Finally, I said, 'Gaz, can we not tell anybody about this?'

Gareth looked relieved. 'Yeah, definitely. I won't say anything.' He gave a big sigh. 'It won't do my reputation with the rugby boys any good if they hear about this.'

'Let's pretend tonight didn't happen,' I said.

Gareth stood up and gave me a small smile. 'Come on, I'll walk you home.'

sOmetImes I'm a BIt NaIve

Me and Ruthie have never been especially close. I think it's because she's five years older than me. Don't get me wrong, I'm not saying that she's loads more mature than I am because she blatantly isn't. She likes to call me things like Fart Face and Blow-off Breath and she paints her Doc Martens in childish colours and wears T-shirts with pictures of *Cookie Monster* printed on the front. There's no way you could ever know, just by looking at her, that my sister Ruthie is actually intelligent. But she is. She got three grade As in her A levels and now she's studying at university so that one day she can be called Dr Ruth Biggs and be widely respected as an expert adviser on archaeological field digs at sites of significant historical interest all over the world.

I don't even know what this means.

Because she's five years older than me, every time I started a new school, Ruthie was just about getting ready to leave it. And then when I got to Year 9, Ruthie cleared off to Aberystwyth and then we weren't even living in the same town any more.

But in spite of all that, there's still some sort of special connection between us. She's the only sister I've got and for one reason or another, we've been through quite a lot together. Goose once told me that she'd love to have a sister like Ruthie and would happily swap both her twin brothers in exchange. And I can sort of see why. Sometimes, Ruthie can be quite generous and gives me her old CDs or something to add to my collection of orang-utan memorabilia. And just this summer, when I went a bit nuts, Ruthie was incredibly nice and understanding and didn't make me feel like I'd let everyone down. In fact, this summer made me appreciate her more than ever and I probably realized for the first time in my life how lucky I am to have an older sister I can talk to. Even if it is usually on the phone.

Which is perhaps why I am still slightly miffed about the fact that she doesn't feel she can open up and talk to me. If she did, she would have told me about Michel. And she would have told me about the things I found in her make-up bag when I got back from the cinema.

I wasn't snooping through her stuff. I was simply looking for some eye make-up remover. And I found some. But I also found these:

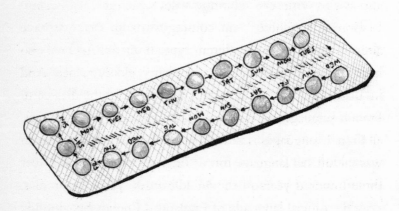

And there were loads of them.

I froze. And then I picked some of them up and looked

at them. And then I froze again. And then I put them back in her make-up bag exactly where I'd found them.

For a couple more minutes, I stood in the bathroom unsure of what to do. Any thoughts of wiping mascara off my eyelashes had completely vanished. Even the shame of my disastrous nudger-prodding date with Gareth was temporarily banished to the back of my mind. The house suddenly seemed so still and so silent that the only thing I could hear was the sound of my own blood as it pumped its way through my head. I put my hands on either side of the sink and leaned against it, breathing deeply inward and outward until the pumping noises in my ears stopped.

Then I left the bathroom and went downstairs.

In the living room, Ruthie, my mum and Michel were drinking wine and talking about France. Michel was saying, 'Actually, in France, we have plenty plenty castles also as you do in this country Wales which is not England. In Bordeaux, where I am coming from, in fact, we have already nine thousand different types of castle. And we also have plenty plenty cheeses and plenty plenty wines. And in Bordeaux, we are speaking a very beautiful dialect of French language which is special of the region. But, in fact, all French languages is beautiful, no? But, of course, French was the official language too of England and Wales for over three hundred years in the Middle Ages, yes? But, in fact, now the official language of England is English but nobody much speaks Welsh in Wales any more, no?'

Ruthie was staring at Michel, utterly transfixed.

Fascination and admiration seemed to be leaking out of her eyes like gunge does from a dodgy old battery. In contrast, my mum looked bored to tears and I could tell that she was really regretting the loss of her *Mamma Mia!* party. When she saw me hanging around in the doorway, she perked right up and said, 'Lottie! How was the film?' Then she patted the empty space next to her on the sofa and said, 'Come and tell us all about it. Was it good?'

'Nah,' I said. Then, looking straight at Ruthie, I said, 'Can I borrow you upstairs for a second?'

Ruthie frowned. 'I'm talking with mum and Michel.'

'I need some help with my computer,' I said.

Ruthie frowned again. 'Now? At this very second?'

My mum said, 'Lottie, you're spending far too much time on that computer.' Then to Ruthie she said, 'It won't kill you to help her. You're not home very often.'

Ruthie looked at Michel and rolled her eyes and then she stood up and said, 'Oh come on then, Fart Face.'

At the top of the stairs, I headed for the bathroom, instead of my bedroom. Ruthie said, 'Where are you going? I thought you wanted me to look at your computer.'

I didn't answer. I walked into the bathroom. Ruthie stood outside and looked confused.

'Please can you come in here a minute?' I said. I was nearly crying.

Ruthie looked alarmed. She followed me into the bathroom and closed the door behind her. Sitting on the edge of the bath, she took hold of both my hands and whispered, 'Lottie, what on earth's the matter?'

And then I started crying. I couldn't help it. I was so freaked out and nervous, I hardly knew what to do with myself. Ruthie said, 'Hey now, it's OK.' And she rubbed my shoulder and smiled reassuringly but all the time I could see that she was really worried.

Finally, once I'd calmed down a bit, I said, 'Why didn't you tell me?'

Ruthie pulled a face which was half a smile and half a look of total bafflement. 'Tell you what?' she asked.

I sniffed and took a deep breath. And then I blurted out, 'TELL ME THAT YOU WERE ILL!'

Ruthie stopped smiling and just looked baffled. 'But I'm not,' she said.

I sniffed again. Now it was my turn to be baffled. 'But you must be,' I said.

'But I'm not,' said Ruthie.

I shook my head. I was starting to get a bit cross with her. 'Don't lie to me, Ruthie. I know you are. Really seriously ill.'

Ruthie looked upset. She took hold of my hands again and said, 'Lottie, sweetheart, listen to me. I'M NOT ILL. NOT AT ALL. THERE IS NOTHING WHATSOEVER WRONG WITH ME.' And then, very gently and very softly, she said, 'But are *you* OK?'

'Yep . . .' I said. And then, 'No.' And then I shook my head, all confused, and said, 'This isn't about me, it's about you!'

'Yes, and I just told you, I'm fine,' said Ruthie.

'THEN WHY HAVE YOU GOT ALL THIS MEDICATION IN YOUR MAKE-UP BAG?' I nearly shouted it and, at the same time, I emptied her make-up bag all over the floor.

Ruthie looked at the tablets which were now by her feet. And then she shut her eyes for a second and sighed. When she opened them again, she said, 'Bloody hell, Lottie! Sometimes you can be so naive!'

'Huh?' I said.

'Have you been snooping through my stuff?'

'No,' I said, nearly crying again. 'I just wanted to use some eye-make up remover and I thought that yours might be more expensive than mine.'

Ruthie sighed again. And then she knelt down on the floor of the bathroom and picked up a strip of tablets. 'Come here,' she said and pulled me down next to her. Slipping one arm around my waist she said, 'These aren't tablets to stop me from dying or anything. It's the Pill.'

It took a few seconds for her words to sink in. My first reaction was one of relief. Even though Ruthie can be annoying, I really wouldn't want her to get horrifically ill. My second reaction was complete and utter mortification.

'Umm, you do *know* what the contraceptive pill is, don't you?' she asked.

'Yes,' I snapped, suddenly shifting into my third reaction – which was total outrage. If I'm honest, I was more outraged with myself for being so stupid than I actually was with

Ruthie for having a sex life but it was far easier to direct my anger at her. 'So you're doing *it* with Michel then?' I hissed. 'And have you been going out with him very long? Do you even know anything much about him? Is this a wise relationship decision, do you think?'

Ruthie gasped in amazement and raised her eyebrows. 'Steady on, Lottie! You're being a bit extreme, aren't you? It's not *actually* any of your business what I do.' And then she pouted and added, 'And I am *twenty* years old, thank you very much, and I haven't entered into all this lightly.' She waved the strip of pills in my face. 'I am taking the necessary precautions.'

I felt my face go very hot. I was furious. Absolutely. Seething. Furious. But only with myself. Because while Ruthie was saying all of this, it occurred to me that despite the fact that I've been unable to think about anything except sex recently, I'd never once thought about the consequences. Which, annoyingly, means that Ruthie is right. I am naive.

In a very disapproving voice, I said, 'Does Mum know?

Ruthie shrugged her shoulders. 'Get real, Lottie. I'm an adult. I don't have to discuss everything with her.'

I bit my thumbnail and thought about this for a moment and then before I could do anything to stop it from happening, I heard a voice ask, 'What's it like?' And, to my absolute and utter horror, it was my voice.

Ruthie, who I think was still a bit annoyed with me, said, '*What?*'

I bit my thumbnail again. Common sense was screaming at me to drop the subject, but I couldn't. I said, 'What does it feel like . . .' I paused, a bit embarrassed, and then whispered, '. . . when you're doing *it*?'

I may as well have asked Ruthie who the prime minister of Luxembourg is. She looked at me in total and utter bewilderment and then, finally, gave a shocked little laugh and said, 'This conversation is TOO WEIRD. Forget it.'

She stood up to go. Panicking, I said, 'I'm not a perv or anything. I'm just curious, that's all!'

Ruthie hesitated and then she said, 'Lottie, you'll find out one day. And when you do, you won't want to go through all the details with *me*, I can promise you that.'

'I'd tell you *anything*,' I said.

Ruthie smiled at me. This time there was no bafflement or amazement or concern in her smile, it was just a really warm and special smile that made me remember why I love her. It also brought me a micro-fraction closer to understanding why Michel might love her too. 'I don't think so,' Ruthie said. 'Not *everything*. There are some things which will always be between you and whoever it is that you fall in love with. But honestly, Lottie, there's loads of time for all of that. Don't be in a rush for it to happen. If you hurry, you might spoil it.'

And then she gave me another lovely smile and made a move to leave. At the door, she paused and said, 'Can we not tell Mum about any of this?'

I gave her a little smile back. 'Let's pretend this conversation didn't happen,' I said.

Ruthie looked grateful. 'Come on, let's go downstairs.'

And I did, and Michel was still droning on and on about France and my mum was still looking about as bored as the most bored person in the whole of Bored-Land and, to be honest, that pretty much sews up yesterday. Which is just as well because if I don't stop typing soon, my fingers will fall off. Blake is right though. Sometimes, writing stuff down helps you to contemplate your life and make some sense of it all. I actually feel a fair bit better now. And if it wasn't for the fact that in precisely two hours I have to be at Gareth's house for Sunday lunch, I'd possibly even feel OK.

QuestIONs I'D LIke aNswereD

A few years ago, Ruthie gave me a book for my birthday which was called *Why Is Snot Green?* I liked that book a lot because it held the answers to some of the really important and intriguing mysteries of life. As well as explaining in very clear detail why snot is such a revolting shade of green, it also shed light on a lot of other interesting worldly phenomena. Stuff like: *Where does all the water go when there's a low tide?* and *Can animals talk?* I read that book from cover to cover and, from its pages, I learned more interesting information than I ever do in an entire year from the boring teachers at school. Earlier this evening, I got that book off my shelf again and had another flip through it. This time it didn't give me the answers I really need. It seems to me that the older you get, the more complicated life becomes and the more difficult it is to find satisfactory responses to the questions that are niggling at you. Questions like:

<u>What does it feel like when you're doing *it*?</u>

Ruthie has already made it categorically clear that she is not going to provide me with the answer to this one. Fat lot of use she is.

<u>Why do I keep saying that Winnie is not keeping me awake every night when, actually, he blatantly is?</u>

In fairness, I am the only person in the entire world who is in a position to answer this question. But even I'm struggling to answer it. Even though I like having Winnie around, I can't say that I appreciate his all-night acrobatics. So why don't I just say something to my mum?

I am a total mystery unto myself. This means that I have something in common with Neil Adam. We are both Welsh enigmas.

<u>Why oh why oh why don't I just say sorry to Goose?</u>

This is one of the most troubling questions of all. I'm sick to the back teeth of the current state of affairs concerning Goose. In all truthfulness, she is one of the funniest and most interesting people I have ever met. We've got so much in common – it's as if we were specifically designed to be best friends with each other. Off the top of my head, these are just some of the similarities we share.

1. We can both recite large chunks of the *Free Willy* film scripts off by heart.
2. We are both highly experimental practitioners of the temporary hair colour application.
3. We both know a lot about shoes.
4. We have both flirted with the philosophy of Existential Absurdism.
5. We have both flirted with Neil Adam aka Mad Alien.
6. We can both eat an entire family bag of marshmallows in under two minutes.
7. We can both say, 'What's cooking in your crazy hot kitchen, baby?' in Welsh.[23]
8. We both think science is deadly dismal.
9. We both, on occasion, like to pretend we're from Kentucky and speak for extended periods of time in fake American accents.
10. We are both very good at speed-walking.

---

[23] *Beth sy'n cwcan yn dy bopty poeth gwyllt, cariad?*

So, frankly, it's utterly ridiculous that we're still not talking to each other. Today, in English, I had to sit next to Goose again and not be her friend for a whole hour and ten minutes. Every single second was terrible and there were four thousand and two hundred of them! What was even worse was that Mr Wood told everyone to work in pairs to answer questions on the nature of friendship in *The Picture of Dorian Gray*. Goose looked at the first question and then, without smiling or seeming in any way interested in hearing my opinion, she said, 'What do you think then?'

I looked at the question. It was this: *Lord Henry says, 'I like to know everything about my new friends and nothing about my old ones.' What does this tell us about Lord Henry?*

'I dunno,' I said and shrugged my shoulders.

'Me neither,' said Goose, and then she said something which sounded like, '*Phrrrphh,*' and put her head on the desk.

I looked at it again and tried to figure it out. After a moment or two, I added, 'I suppose it means that Lord Henry is a shallow, backbiting idiot because he bins off his old friends in favour of his new ones.'

Goose sat up and gave me a hard look. 'What's that supposed to mean?'

'Nothing,' I said.

Goose gave me another hard look. Eventually she said, 'Or maybe it just tells us that Lord Henry is more interested in his new friends because his old ones are boring and selfish.'

I felt myself getting annoyed. I said, 'What exactly are you trying to say, Gail?'

Goose said, 'I'm not exactly trying to say anything, Charlotte.'

'Well, don't then,' I said.

'Well, I won't,' she answered.

'Well, good then,' I said.

'Well, whatever,' said Goose.

And then we both just sat and didn't speak to each other for the whole lesson and just answered the questions by ourselves. By the time the bell rang, I'd finished all of them. I don't think I've ever worked so hard in my entire life. Mr Wood was really impressed and gave us each a merit mark. I wasn't really that fussed by mine. In fact, I'd have happily shoved that poxy merit mark up his backside if it meant that things could go back to how they used to be. Once upon a time, me and Goose used to be far too busy messing about to get merit marks. To be honest, I really miss her. Which is why I suppose I ought to say sorry.

But since yesterday, all these perplexing puzzles have had to take a back seat in my head because the question which has really been puzzling me is this one:

<u>Why do boys' bedrooms smell of wood?</u>

All boys' bedrooms smell of wood. This is not an opinion. It's a fact. I'd even go as far as to say it's an olfactory fact! Sometimes it's a pungent woody smell like our oak kitchen table, and other times it's more of a general woody aroma like the smell of trees in a forest. Then again, sometimes it's quite a whiffy woody smell like you get from the dirty wood shavings at the bottom of a hamster's cage. I have no idea what actually causes this wood-smelling phenomenon. I can only think that it stems from a gaseous substance which radiates naturally out of boys' bodies. Girls' rooms are very different. Take my room, for example. Even though I've got an elderly chinchilla living in my room in a cage containing sawdust and sand, he doesn't make my room smell funny. In actual fact, it's the other way round. My room has made Winnie smell nice. This morning I picked up Winnie and sniffed him all over and I couldn't detect anything except faint hints of hairspray and *Impulse*. I'm quite sure that Winnie wouldn't be so sweetly fragrant if he was living in a boy's room.

All boys' rooms have that woody whiff. Goose's twin brothers, Bill and James, share a big bedroom and it absolutely reeks of wood. The smell of it hits you, like a gigantic toppling Canadian Redwood, as soon as you open the door. I wouldn't even be surprised if Goose's dad has to paint their walls with creosote to stop them from going all mushy and rotten. Then there's my little brother, Caradoc. His bedroom still has quite a babyish aroma about it but, even so, during my last visit to Wrexham, I'm sure I could detect the very beginnings of the woody smell taking hold in his bedroom. It also smells a little bit of wee. Now I'm thinking about it, I really wish it had occurred to me to ask

Ruthie about the room that Michel sleeps in. It's too late now because they both got the bus back to Aberystwyth last night but I'm prepared to bet all the money in the world that this woody smell is not merely a feature of British males and their bedrooms. I bet Michel's room smells like a French forest filled with fuggy fir trees.

Gareth's bedroom smells a bit like our garden fence. It's not unpleasant but there's definitely a scent of outdoors and also a hint of something quite sturdy and practical hanging in the air. It's the same kind of smell I sniff when my mum drags me into the DIY store to buy door handles and coat hooks.

Until yesterday, I'd never actually been in Gareth's house and I certainly hadn't been in his bedroom. To be honest, the prospect of seeing where Gareth eats and sleeps and does all his other private personal business had been making me feel a bit nervous. I mean, what if his house was really freaky! But it's also been making me feel incredibly nosy, so by the time I actually got to go round there, I could hardly even wait for Gareth to open the front door. It was all I could do to stop myself from barging right past him so that I could start having a good look round. I was expecting it all to be a bit scruffy like The Jean Genie hair salon. But actually it isn't. Although my mum wouldn't like me to say it, his house is a lot tidier than ours. Everywhere is completely shiny and spotless. Even Gareth's bedroom looked as if it had been recently tidied up. I couldn't spot a single dirty coffee mug anywhere in his entire room and, currently, I think there are about five in mine. Gareth's walls are painted dark blue and mostly covered in framed posters of U2 and the Welsh rugby team. All his rugby books are neatly arranged in order of height on a metal shelf screwed to the wall and all his rugby DVDs are displayed on a wire stand which is shaped like a saxophone. His bed is covered in a duvet which has a giant Welsh flag printed on it and he has a rug and curtains which match. Everything is so completely tidy that when I saw it, I was a bit spooked. 'Nice room, Gaz,' I said as I perched awkwardly on the end of his Welsh dragon bed and then, for no reason that I can remember, I glanced upward. On the ceiling, right above my head, was a massive poster of Britney Spears wearing nothing but a skimpy gold bra and skimpy gold hot pants. It gave me a bit of a shock. I suppose I'm not very used to boys' bedrooms. I said, 'So you're a Britney fan, then, Gareth? Or is it your dad's?'

Gareth looked up at the ceiling and turned bright red. Then he said, 'Oh yeah, that! My mum won't let him put it up in their bedroom so he just shoved it on the ceiling in here to keep it out of the way.'

Gareth is very sweet but he does occasionally underestimate my common sense.

Gareth's mum was downstairs cooking us a roast turkey lunch. When I'd walked past the dining room earlier, I'd caught a glimpse of a table laid with napkins and candles. Our dining table only ever looks like that at Christmas. 'Wow!' I'd said. 'My mum usually makes our Sunday lunch from a packet mix and we have it on our laps while we're watching the telly.'

Jean Stingecombe had laughed and said, 'Nothing's too much trouble for my Gazzy and his young lady, is it, Mick?'

Mick Stingecombe is Gareth's dad. He's even bigger and beefier than Gareth and he has a bristly white head and a thick neck. When I arrived, he was wearing a Welsh dragon apron and making Yorkshire puddings. He didn't look like a Britney Spears fan. He said, 'No, Jean,' and smiled at us.

Jean said, 'We're delighted to have you for lunch, aren't we, Mick?'

Gareth's dad said, 'Yes, Jean.'

Jean Stingecombe laughed and said, 'Gazzy hasn't ever brought a girlfriend home before, has he, Mick?'

Gareth's dad said, 'No, Jean.'

As we were walking up the stairs to his bedroom, Gareth said, 'I told you my parents would be embarrassing. They're perfectly harmless though.'

From the kitchen, I heard Jean Stingecombe say, 'Can I trust you with those Yorkshire puds, Mick?'

And I heard Gareth's dad say, 'Yes, Jean.'

'Does your dad say anything other than yes and no?' I whispered.

'Oh yeah,' laughed Gareth. 'Occasionally. If you're very lucky, you might hear him say something else, later.'

In the privacy of his fence-smelling bedroom and underneath the Britney Spears poster, I said, 'I'm sorry about last night, Gaz.'

Gareth said, 'Forget about it. It wasn't your fault.'

'Wasn't it?' I said hopefully.

'Nah. I'd pigged out on too much junk. Coach Jenkins reckons we've got to learn to enjoy pleasure in moderation if any of us are going to make it as professional rugby players.'

We sat side by side on his bed quietly thinking about this. From downstairs, the smell of roast dinner was wafting through the house and mingling with the fencey smell of Gareth's room. Gareth got up from the bed and closed the door. 'Keep the smell out,' he said.

He sat back down next to me on the bed.

'When will lunch be ready?' I said.

''bout another half an hour,' said Gareth.

He reached over and put his hand on top of mine. Almost immediately, my heart started thumping so hard that it felt like it was actually going to thump its way right out of my body. It was thumping so loudly that I could hear it. I sat there, on the fiery Welsh dragon, underneath Britney Spears, with my heart going thump thump thump thump thump and I couldn't hear another sound in the entire room. The silence was so intense it was making my ears ache.

Gareth said, 'Shall I stick a CD on?'

'Good idea,' I said gratefully.

He got up and put a U2 CD on his stereo and turned the volume right up loud. The first song to come blaring out of the speakers was very noisy and the kind of thing which the boys in my school like to jump up and down to at school discos as if they are trying to qualify for the Stunt Pogo Olympics. It was still better than listening to that terrible ear-splitting silence though. 'What is this?' I said. To be honest, I wasn't really that interested. I was just making small talk.

'Vertigo,' said Gareth. 'It's my favourite ever U2 single.'

'Vertigo?' I said. 'I don't even know what that means.'

Gareth scratched his head. 'It's like being dizzy. This record is so amazing it makes me go a bit dizzy sometimes.' He came back and sat on the bed. And then, without any warning, he kissed me. It lasted forty-three seconds. Actually, it probably lasted a bit longer than that because I was caught off guard and I didn't start counting from the point of initial lip contact.

On the forty-fourth second I pulled away for an oxygen intake. Once I'd got my breath back, I rested my hand on the back of his neck and whispered, 'Gareth, did you think any more about what I said yesterday?'

'You mean about *it*?' Gareth whispered back, looking visibly shocked. 'I'm not doing *it* NOW with my parents downstairs. And anyway it'll be dinner in a little while and I need at least an hour when I'm doing *it*.'

'How do you know?' I whispered back to him. 'You said you've never done *it* before.'

Gareth pulled away from me, looking faintly annoyed. 'Yeah, well, I know enough about myself to know that I'm the sort of person *not* to rush an important job like that,' he said. 'I like to do things properly.'

The music was still shaking the speakers of Gareth's stereo. 'OK,' I said. 'Kiss me slowly and properly then. That other kiss only lasted forty-three poxy seconds.'

Gareth looked at me in amazement and then he said, 'You're mad you are, Lottie Biggs.' The second he'd said that, he put his hand to his mouth and said, 'Ooh, sorry! No offence, like.'

But I wasn't offended because, actually, I *was* feeling a little bit mad. But in a good way. From the speakers, Bono from U2 was shouting about how he was in a place called Vertigo and I understood what he meant because I felt like I was right there with him. All of a sudden, I was feeling really high up and dizzy and as eerily cheerily chipper as a chirpy bouncing chinchilla. I felt like I could have bounced right up to the ceiling if I'd wanted to. I laughed and tickled Gareth. Gareth tickled me back. I giggled and notched my tickling up a gear. Gareth responded by tickling me even harder. The next thing I knew, we were wriggling around on his Welsh dragon duvet and giggling and covering each other's faces in little kisses and, all the while, Britney Spears was looking down on us from above. But I didn't even care about her. She's got no chance with Gareth. She lives in America.

Then, halfway through the song, the music stopped.

Gareth and I instantly froze. Gareth was kneeling on top of me with one hand about to tickle my tummy, now nakedly visible because my sweatshirt had ridden upward, and the other hand resting on my sweatshirt-covered boob. In return,

I had both my hands jammed into the back pockets of his jeans and was clutching hold of his denim-covered cheeks. It was what the newspapers would call *a compromising position*.

I heard a cough and then Gareth's dad said, 'I did knock, Gareth. Repeatedly. But obviously, you didn't hear. When you've finished there, son, would you bring Lottie down to lunch.' And then he left the room.

For a couple of minutes we sat on Gareth's bed in absolute silence. Finally, Gareth said, 'I told you he sometimes says a bit more than yes and no.' And then, because I didn't have the courage to run away, I pulled my sweatshirt down, got off the bed and followed him down the stairs.

Which brings me to my final question.

<u>Will I ever again be able to eat Yorkshire puddings
without feeling totally mortified?</u>

BeING fraNk wIth BLake

'It's been a funny old couple of weeks,' I said to Blake. 'To be honest, I'm not sure how successful I've been at surfing that cosmic wave.'

'Why's that then?' he asked.

I thought about his question and frowned. Opposite me, Blake sat patiently in his swivel chair and waited. Inside my head, I tried to untangle all the emotional things which had happened since my last visit but it was quite difficult because there was an awful lot to untangle. Everything seemed to have got twisted together like spaghetti. After a minute or two of silence, I took a deep breath and said, 'Well, since I saw you last, I've totally fallen out with my best friend Goose, almost been sacked from my Saturday job, told fifty billion fibs to my mum, been driven to distraction by a pair of Britney Spears boxer shorts, developed an allergy to Yorkshire puddings, got myself practically thrown out of the cinema for being a prodder, nearly shoved a merit mark up my English teacher's backside and shouted my head off about being a great big virgin in the middle of the high street.'

Blake raised his eyebrows and said, 'Get off the grass!'

'No, I'm deadly serious,' I said.

Blake frowned a little and nodded. 'Anything else?'

I thought about it. Then I said, 'Do you want more?'

Blake shrugged. 'Do you want to tell me more?'

I put my head on one side and thought about this and

then I said, 'Can I be frank with you, Blake?'

Blake held out his palms. 'Be as frank as you like.'

'Well,' I said, 'the thing is – see – I've got this boyfriend called Gareth and we're in a proper relationship and he's really nice – I mean really REALLY nice – and in the past, I've thought other boys were nice but – actually – none of them are as nice as Gareth is because he's EXTREMELY nice – and he's so nice that – initially – I thought it would be nicer if we both waited until we were about twenty-one before we did the Grand Slam – don't ask me why, I suppose I just thought that it would make the experience EVEN nicer – but then the other day, I caught a glimpse of Gaz in his Britney Spears boxer shorts and he looked SOOO nice – I mean SOOO COMPLETELY SEXADELICALLY SCRUMPTIOUSLY NICE that – to be honest – I can't stop thinking about him and now – the truth is – I can't be blinking bothered to hang around until I'm twenty-blinking-one before I do the Wham Bam Grand Slam with him because I WANT TO DO IT WITH HIM RIGHT NOW – well, I don't mean *RIGHT* NOW – obviously – because Gareth isn't here and this room would be a TOTALLY inappropriate and blatantly weird venue for that kind of activity but I DEFINITELY WANT TO DO IT SOMETIME SOON – but the problem is that Gareth is SO NICE that he wants everything to be completely perfect and while I agree that it would be a lot nicer if we had plenty of space and privacy and time to relax and no parents about to barge in – actually, now I think about it, that is essential – I DEFINITELY don't want any parents barging in – but – what was I saying? – oh yeah – I'm beginning to wonder when it's EVER GOING TO HAPPEN and – I'll be honest – the entire situation is keeping me awake at night – well, so is Winnie but he's an elderly chinchilla so that's completely different – and – actually – I haven't had a decent night's sleep for ages now because all I can think about is the fact that I'M DESPERATE TO DO *IT* WITH GARETH STINGECOMBE and it's all starting to cave my head in and – I can tell you now – that's not nice.'

When I'd finished, I took a few deep breaths and gripped the armrests of my chair to steady myself. At some point during all of this, I'd started rocking backwards and forward a little bit.

Blake sat up a little straighter in his seat and stroked his chin. I'm not sure if I was imagining things but his face seemed to have gone a little pinker than usual. After a while, he said, 'Crikey dick! That WAS frank!'

'You said I could be,' I said.

Blake nodded in agreement. 'That's fine, Lottie. Frank is good.' Then after a pause, he added, 'Aside from all of this, how would you describe your general day-to-day mood?'

I shrugged. And then I said, 'Recently? Pretty good actually. I feel quite chirpy and buzzy. I kind of feel like I'm in a place called Vertigo.'

Blake frowned slightly and then he said, 'Hmm.'

We sat for a moment without saying anything. Blake,

who is generally quite a relaxed and smiley person, was looking extremely thoughtful. Not unlike this:

© Jag Gundu / BEI / Rex Features

After a little while, he said, 'Is Vertigo a good place to be?'

This is one of the things I really like about Blake. Even though he's a mental health counsellor and sometimes uses weird words all the way from New Zealand, essentially we speak the same lingo.

I scratched my head and probably looked as thoughtful as he did. Then I said, 'I think so. Most of the time. When I'm not packing a wobbly. It can be quite exciting and I definitely don't feel bored and I GET LOADS OF STUFF DONE. I mean, I've already written about forty thousand words for my Emotion Notepad. Are you sure you don't want to read it?'

Blake said, 'Get off the grass! FORTY THOUSAND WORDS!'

'Yep,' I said with a nod. 'There's just been so much stuff happening.'

And then Blake said, 'Do you feel normal though?'

And I looked at him and opened my mouth to answer the question but not a sound came out because I couldn't think of a single word to say. Instead, my whole head was being held hostage by one solitary mind–bending question. It was this question:

What *is* normal?

And I sat in my seat and started thinking about all of the people I know. I thought about Lee Fogel who is always horrible to me and I thought, 'Is *he* normal?' And then I thought about Dilys who eats three bags of mint humbugs every day and I thought, 'Is *she* normal?' And then I thought about Ruthie who has a freaky interest in old bones and broken bits of pottery and I asked myself, 'Is *Ruthie* normal?' And to be honest, I just felt even more confused.

Eventually I said, 'But what the blinking heck is normal?'

Blake smiled. 'That, Lottie, is a humdinger of a question. And one I can't really answer because we all wear different gumboots, don't we? And it's a cracking good job that we do because life would be pretty dull otherwise. I suppose what I'm really asking is if this is how you *normally* feel?'

'Oh,' I said. And then I added, 'No, not really. Usually, I can't be bothered to get loads of stuff done. To be honest, I've got a naturally lazy streak.'

'Have you been in this Vertigo place before?' asked Blake.

I shifted about a bit on my seat. All of a sudden, no matter how much I wriggled and squirmed around, I couldn't quite rid myself of the sensation that I was sitting on the most uncomfortable chair in the entire cosmos. But just as I was starting to feel that the only way ahead would be to pick up the stupid comfortless chair and throw it through the flaming window, I was struck head-on by a colossal realization.

I *HAD* BEEN HERE BEFORE.

Just before I'd had my mental disturbance in the summer.

Just before it all went dark and depressing.

Blake smiled. 'Wearing different gumboots to the rest of the crowd isn't always a bad thing, you know. Not everyone can thump out forty thousand words like you can. Buzzy episodes can be extremely productive. I've heard lots of people say that they wouldn't ever want to be without them – even if it means taking the rough with the smooth. But it's important to spot when you're having a buzzy phase because you know what might be following hot on its heels, don't you?'

I nodded. 'A big fat non-buzzy downer.'

'Spot on, sport,' said Blake with a wink. 'And once you know when it could be coming, you're in a better position to cope with it.'

I bit my thumbnail and frowned. Blake's words had got me thinking. To be honest, I'm *still* thinking about them and it's twenty to one in the morning and I really should be asleep. I'm not sure how any of this helps me solve my personal problems with Goose and Gareth but I do know that the thought of going through another big fat miserable depression like the one I had in the summer scares me half to death.

After a while I said very quietly, 'Am I gonna be OK?'

Blake smiled at me again and it was one of those smiles which makes you feel better just for seeing it. I don't think I could have felt any better if Johnny Depp himself had smiled at me. Blake said, 'Try to be patient. Your nervous system has been really crook, Lottie, and it's got to recover. You know, it might even be that some of these jiggy feelings you've got for Gareth are just another symptom of everything still being a bit haywire. Or maybe not.' Then he looked a bit pink again. 'But, either way, it always takes a little time to control the ups and downs. Just keep working on the techniques we've talked about and you'll soon learn how to keep your balance.'

'Should I keep writing in my Emotion Notepad?' I asked.

'Does it help?' said Blake.

I nodded vigorously. 'Definitely,' I said. 'It kind of feels like I've got a twenty-four-hour hotline to someone who's got bigger ears and more patience and a calmer personality than even Yoda from *Star Wars*, and he's a Jedi Master,' and then I added, 'if you know what I mean.'

Yoda looks like this:

Which is actually not a million miles away from what Winnie my chinchilla looks like. And Winnie's not a bad listener either.

Blake must have seen the *Star Wars* films too because he said, 'Crikey Dick! Keep writing then. But don't forget to give yourself a break from that screen sometimes. And try not to write at freaky hours in the morning. A well rested mind is a healthy mind.'

And then his alarm clock went off.

'That's my lot then,' I said and stood up and walked over to the door. Before I left though, I paused and said, 'You're a great listener as well, Blake.'

Blake grinned again. 'Hey, bugalugs, I'm just doing my job.'

I grinned back. 'Yeah, well, thanks, bugalugs.' And then I left.

And now I'm switching my computer off and going to sleep because if I've learned one important thing today, it's this:

Even though we all wear different gumboots, sitting in front of your computer in the freaky hours of the morning just isn't healthy or normal.

hOw Gareth stINGeCOmBe OffereD Me hIs sausaGe

This morning I arrived to work at The Jean Genie hair salon at a sensible time. Just for once, I wasn't stupidly early. There's no danger of this situation ever repeating itself though. Because I've decided that I'm going to resign. I haven't told my mum yet and now she's gone out for the evening so I can't tell her anyway, and I haven't told Gareth yet because he doesn't actually deserve to know this piece of exclusive news. The sad truth is that he'd rather put a wiggly maggot on a hook than spend time alone in my house with me. And I can't tell Goose because Goose doesn't like me. So that just leaves me with the Emotion Notepad and Winnie.

So here goes . . .

As usual, I woke up ages before my alarm and I could tell from the lack of light shining through the curtains that it was still dark outside. Even though I'd only been awake for a few seconds, my brain was already buzzing and whirring like a demented fridge. I didn't want to stay in bed so I got up and transferred myself to my wardrobe. While I was in there, I closed my eyes and forced myself to count imaginary orang-utans as they swung from one treetop to the next. The first few hundred orang-utans were a bit uptight and edgy but by the time I'd reached my target of three thousand ginger swingers, they were feeling a lot more relaxed and so was I. After that, I played with Winnie for a bit and then I had a long hot shower. Downstairs, I made myself a big special breakfast of sardines on toast followed by two oranges and a banana. In the summer, I had several appointments with Dr Edwards and she told me that fruit, vegetables and oily fish are very good for everyone – but especially for people like me who have vulnerable heads. To be honest, I'm not very keen on vegetables – unless you count chips – but I don't mind the odd bit of fruit or the occasional oily fish.[24]

When I got to work, Dilys was opening her first bag of mint humbugs and Neil Adam was taking off his avant-garde plastic leopard-print raincoat. Jean looked up from the appointments book and said, 'Hiya, Lottie! Not such an early bird this morning. But you're still nice and punctual and there's nothing quite as useful in this life as the trick of good timing, is there, my lovely?'

'No,' I said. 'It's a much better way to operate.' I wasn't making small talk either. I totally meant it.

Dilys said, 'Oooh Lottie, did you enjoy your lunch around at Jean's last Sunday?

My cheeks INSTANTLY started burning. I looked from Dilys to Jean and then back again to Dilys but I couldn't see anything sly or disapproving in either of their faces. They were both just smiling at me quite innocently. With a secret sigh of relief, I realized that Gareth's dad probably hadn't told Jean about the boob and cheeks tickling incident. I said, 'Yeah, it was nice thanks, Dilys.'

---

[24] Except for Lee Fogel.

Dilys said, 'Oooh, Jean's Mick can make a mean Yorkshire pud, can't he?'

'Hmm,' I said and then, to change the subject, I asked, 'Do anything interesting last night, Neil?'

Neil said, 'Went to a club. Had a few women throw themselves at me. The usual.'

I quite like Neil but it's no wonder that things never worked out between him and Goose. She might think she's as tasty as a bar of chocolate but Neil thinks he's an entire Cadbury's factory.

Dilys said, 'Oooh, fighting off the ladies again then, Neily?'

Neil said, 'None of them floated my boat, Dil.' And then he winked at me and made my face go hot again.

Jean had switched the CD player on and was now turning the sign on the door to *Open*. As she walked back to the reception desk, the speakers crackled into life and she began humming along to the song which was playing. It was the same song which is almost always playing.

Before I could stop myself, I said, 'Jean, can't we listen to something else today? Not this same drippy love song over and over again?'

Jean gave a little laugh but she actually looked a bit shocked. With her hands on her hips and her head tilted sharply to one side, she said, 'You do exaggerate, Lottie! It's not *one* song. It's a whole album of *wonderful* songs.'

I sighed. 'Yeah, I appreciate that,' I said, trying really hard not to cause any more offence, '. . . but it's a bit . . . well . . . boring.'

Jean raised her eyebrows. 'Boring? It's NOT BORING. Carole King's *Tapestry* is the thirty-sixth greatest album EVER made. That's a fact, Lottie! Ask anyone.'

'Is it?' I asked Neil.

Neil shrugged his shoulders and said, 'I'd never actually heard of it before I came to work here. But to be fair, I only really listen to George Michael.'

Jean shook her head and looked exasperated. 'You kids! Honestly! You can't recognize a lovely tune even when it's right inside your lugholes. But even my Gazzy loves this album.'

'Does he?' I asked in surprise.

'Absolutely *adores* it,' said Jean. 'Bless his little heart.'

I sighed. I was starting to feel a bit colossally confused. I'm still a bit colossally confused by that fact even now. Me and Gareth Stingecombe are usually on exactly the same wavelength. What can he possibly hear in this stupid boring middle-aged music that I can't? Not wanting to give up the fight, I argued, 'But it doesn't even make any sense. What on earth does she *mean* when she whines on about feeling like an *actual* woman? What other kind of woman is there?'

Jean laughed. 'You've misheard it, Lottie, sweetheart. It's not *actual* she's saying – it's NATURAL. I suppose she's telling her man that he makes her feel strong – strong enough to own up to the fact that she's a *normal natural* human being who sometimes makes mistakes and needs his understanding and support from time to time. I, personally, think it's a very beautiful song.' And then she added, 'And Dilys loves it and the clients love it, so I'm afraid, Lottie, you're just going to have to lump it.' She stuck her tongue out at me and got up to greet Mrs Lewis who comes in every Saturday just to have a wash and blow-dry. I sighed and picked up the broom. Jean can be a bit childish sometimes. She's still got the power to beat me in every argument though.

A few minutes before my lunch hour, just as I was out the back loading wet towels into the washing machine, Neil popped his head through the doorway and said, 'There's a great big hunk of chunk to see you.'

'You're starting to sound like Dilys,' I warned him.

'Oooh, do you think so?' he said. And then he winked at me and started laughing like a donkey.

Gareth was waiting on the pavement outside the salon. When he saw me, he smiled and said, 'I'm treating you to whatever you fancy from *Pat's Plaice*. I reckon it must be hard work being in there all day with that scatty womanizer, Mad Alien.'

'Neil's all right,' I said and linked my arm through Gareth's. 'I just don't think he's found what he's looking for yet.'

Gareth scowled. 'Yeah, well, so long as he doesn't try to find it by making any moves on you.'

I laughed. 'You just don't get it, do you, Gaz?'

'Get what?' said Gareth.

We'd come to a halt outside the chip shop. I took hold of his hand and right in the middle of Whitchurch village, I said, 'Why would I keep going on about wanting to do *it* with you if there was *any* possibility that I might be interested in Neil Adam?'

Gareth smiled a bit and said, 'Oh!'

'Honestly, Gaz,' I said, 'you don't have to worry about anyone else flirting with me because you're the only person I fancy in the whole of Whitchurch.'

Gareth looked up and down the crappy high street. A slight look of confusion clouded his face. 'Oh?'

'I mean in the whole of Cardiff,' I added quickly. And then, just to make sure I was really getting my point across, I said, 'Well, in the whole of anywhere, really.'

Gareth beamed and said, 'Oh!'

For a moment, we stood outside *Pat's Plaice,* just looking into each other's eyes and holding hands. I could smell the delicious smell of the chip shop wafting up my nostrils and it was like a giant Lottie magnet trying to pull me in through its doors. But right then, there wasn't one single thing on the planet which could have enticed me to move. If I had a pause button which could freeze me forever at one specific moment in time, I'd have pressed it right then.

But then Lee Fogel came out of the chip shop stuffing a pickled egg into his big mouth and the moment evaporated.

Gareth pulled me into the chippy and we bought our food. As it wasn't raining, we took it outside so that we could sit on the ledge under the window and eat it. For a few minutes we sat there side by side, munching chips and saying nothing. Across the street, Goose and Spud appeared from the doorway of the Dragon Coffee House. They were holding hands and Goose had Spud's rugby shirt draped across her shoulders. It looked rubbish. They stood outside the cafe and had a great big smoochy pashy and then Spud looked up and waved at Gareth. Goose looked down at the ground. I watched as they walked further up the street and stopped by the traffic island to chat to a group of sixth-formers I didn't know. Goose obviously knew them though. I could see that they were all having a right old laugh about something.

I tapped my heels up and down against the pavement so that they made a really fast CLICK CLICK CLICK sound and said, 'Have you thought about *it* any more?'

Gareth frowned and licked his chippy fingers. Then he said, 'Yeah. Course I have. I keep on thinking about what you said in the Ponty-Carlo. I can't actually think about anything else.'

'Me neither,' I said. And then I took a deep breath and added, 'My mum is going out for a meal with her friends tonight. I'm gonna have the place all to myself.' My heels were still going CLICK CLICK CLICK.

Gareth picked up a chip and said, 'Oh.'

'We'll need to be properly prepared though,' I said. 'You know, do *it* responsibly.'

Gareth put down his chip and stared at the pavement between his feet. Then, after several million light years had passed, he lifted his head and said, 'The thing is, see, it's a bit difficult.'

'Difficult?' I said. My heels stopped clicking.

'Yeah,' nodded Gareth. 'Difficult. Coach Jenkins reckons that unnecessary expenditure of energy could be detrimental to my overall performance on the field of play.'

'Huh?' I said.

Gareth looked round to see that there was nobody within earshot and then, in a low voice, he said, 'Basically, I reckon that he must mean no shagging before a big game.'

'But you haven't got any big games coming up, have you?' I asked.

Gareth, who was already quite pink, flushed ultra-pink. 'But I *might* have, Lottie. You never know when you're going to get that call to play for the Wales youth team, you really don't. It could come at *any* time.' He ate another chip and then added, 'Besides, I said I'd go night fishing with Spud this evening.'

'You'd rather go *fishing* with Spud than come round to my mum-less house?' I said.

Gareth frowned again. 'He's my best mate. I haven't done anything with him for ages.'

I sighed and felt a bit stroppy. And then I remembered what Blake said about my haywire nervous system and tried to chill out a bit.

Gareth said, 'Next week would be better for me, it really would.'

Before I could stop myself, I said, 'Yeah, but *when* next week? I thought you *might* have a big rugby match.'

Gareth bit his lip. I think he was feeling harassed. And

I think it was me who was doing the harassing. I can be a real witch sometimes, I really can. I was just on the very brink of apologizing, when Gareth looked me right in the eye and said in a firm voice, '*You* are more important to me than rugby. I wish you'd understand that.' He bit his lip again, before adding, 'Why don't you come round Tuesday night? My mum and dad are going line dancing. They won't be back before ten.' And then he looked down at his food and went quiet. I suppose I hadn't actually expected him to say all this because I was suddenly completely lost for words. But then, Gareth broke the awful pause anyway and said, 'You know what? I don't really fancy all of this now.' He nodded downward. 'My eyes have been bigger than my belly again.' He speared his untouched jumbo sausage with his white plastic fork and then, with the faintest hint of a grin, he waved it under my nose and said, 'Fancy my sausage, do you, babe?'

severaL shOCkING reveLatIONs

I know it's not for me to say but I think I've always been fairly clever. Apart from in maths, science, geography, French, Welsh, business studies and RE, I've mostly managed to do quite well in tests, and when it comes to English and history, I'm usually near the top of the class. Once, when I was ten, I won third prize in a short story competition organized by my bank[25] and then, when I was twelve, I came second in my school spelling competition. And let's not forget that my last piece of English coursework was a perfect A★ – whereas Goose only managed to get an A. Anyone with this list of achievements under their belt can't be entirely stupid.

And yet sometimes I can't see the truth even when it's standing right in front of me and staring me straight in the face. Sometimes, the truth has to bash me over the head with a sledgehammer before I can see things as they actually and truly are. When this happens, it's a very freaky and discombobulating experience. There's no time to get to grips with a new idea – it's just there. Instantly. Like an email. Mr Wood, my English teacher, would describe this experience as *a shocking revelation*. Shocking revelations can really knock you sideways.

---

[25] I had to write a story which began with the words: *Billy was so pleased that he had opened a new bank account*. It wasn't easy to make anything interesting out of that beginning, but I think all the stuff about Billy being a brain-eating zombie gave my story added depth.

This afternoon, in The Jean Genie, I scored a hat-trick. I had three of them.

The first shocking revelation came at the end of my lunch break. I'd already said goodbye to Gareth and was making my way back to the salon when I saw Lee Fogel and Samantha Morgan hanging around by the bus shelter. Lee was eating another pickled egg, or at least, I assume he was. Perhaps he's actually the slowest pickled egg-eater in the world and it was the same one. When he saw me, he took his egg out of his gob and said, 'Hello, Potty. Tempera*mental* weather we're having today, don't you think?'

Lee Fogel is such an idiot.

I carried on walking.

Lee called out after me, 'Oi, Potty! Me and Sam were just discussing a few environ*mental* issues.'

I carried on walking.

Lee Fogel called out even louder, 'Stingecombe likes a bit of fun with a *mental*, does he?'

I stopped. And then, almost like I was being operated by a remote control somewhere, I turned around and walked back to the bus shelter. 'What did you say?' I said.

Lee Fogel sneered at me and shrugged his shoulders. 'I just said that Stingecombe is funda*mentally* a nice guy. What's wrong with that?'

'Nothing's wrong with that,' I said. 'But you know what, Lee? I think you're just a mindless little *dick*ybird who needs to look up the word mental in the *dick*tionary before you start *dick*tating your stupid ideas to me. Because, guess what? I don't give a *Dick*ens what you think!'

It wasn't brilliant but I think I made my feelings about him clear. I was upset though. My heart was thumping so hard that I'm surprised I didn't break a rib.

Lee Fogel stopped sneering and turned downright nasty. 'You don't give a *Dick*ens? What's that supposed to mean, Nut-Nut?'

My eyes had suddenly gone all watery and my whole body was trembling. I bit my lip and tried to stop myself from crying but it was really difficult. A few tears leaked out anyway and my jaw was wobbling dangerously. I said, 'I just think . . . I just think . . .' And then I stopped because I didn't want Lee Fogel to hear my voice go all squeaky and pathetic.

Samantha Morgan, who'd been studying the bus timetable, turned round and said, 'She thinks you're a dickhead, Lee, and, do you know what? So do I.'

Me and Lee both looked at Samantha in surprise. In fact, I was so surprised I forgot to be upset. It was as if I'd just woken up after being bashed painlessly on the head and was now seeing the world from a completely new perspective. Samantha shrugged and said, 'I can't help it, Lee. I say what I see and from where I'm standing I can see a total and utter arse.'

Lee gawped at Samantha and said, 'What?' And then he said, 'Whose side are you on anyway, you dopey woman?'

Samantha scratched her chin and pretended to think about it. After a couple of nanoseconds, she said, 'Right now, Lee, I'm on Lottie's side.'

Lee continued to gawp at her.

I was gawping at her too. 'I thought you didn't like me,' I said. My jaw had stopped wobbling and I was miraculously able to speak again.

Samantha rolled her eyes. 'Get over it, Lottie! That was ages ago. I'm sorry about that time I called your mum a rozzer—'

'I thought you said *lezzer*,' I said really quickly.

'Whatever,' said Samantha Morgan. '*Rozzer? Lezzer?* Does it actually matter any more? It was stupid anyway.' She jerked her head at Lee Fogel and added, 'But one thing I *do* know is that I've had enough of standing around watching *you* being vile to people. So consider yourself dumped.'

And then she crossed over the road and disappeared in the direction of the flyover, leaving me and Lee Fogel just standing there.

I stood up as tall and straight as I could. I wasn't shaking any more. Lee Fogel had gone very red and his mouth was hanging open. In my very best sarcastic voice, I said, 'Oh dear – what a pity – never mind!' And then I walked back to the salon feeling extremely pleased.

Which just leaves me to summarise my Shocking Revelation Number One: Samantha Morgan is actually a very decent person. The sad truth is that once upon a time we used to hang out together but now we don't. And I'm extremely concerned that my friendship with Goose could end up going the same way.

Shocking Revelation Number Two came shortly afterwards when Neil and I were sitting together behind the reception desk and looking at the latest issue of *Hair Necessities*. The salon was quieter than usual and, to give him something to do, Jean had told Neil to help me with the appointments book and the telephone enquiries. To be honest, I didn't actually need any help with either. No one was coming in from the street to book an appointment and the telephone wasn't ringing at all. So, instead, we just sat and looked through all the hair magazines. In the background, Jean's favourite Carole King CD was playing just like it always is. Neil was searching the pages of *Hair Necessities* for a good example of a Caesar haircut and crooning along softly to the natural woman song.

I tapped my finger on a picture of a male model with his hair all brushed upward into a Mohawk fin and said, 'How about something like that next time, Neil? That would look really good on you.'

Neil studied the picture and, after a pause, said, 'I'm not sure. I think my face is too square to be able to carry that particular style. If you look at the model, he's got a cherub-like face – rather like an upside-down teardrop – whereas my face is much more angular. No, I don't think I could wear that style.'

I shrugged my shoulders and said, 'Well, *I* think it would suit you.'

Neil pushed the magazine away from him and looked at me. I noticed he had that same dirty twinkle in his eye that he has every time he's about to say something inappropriate to Dilys. He said, 'Do you think it would make me sexually *irresistible* though, Lottie?'

I felt myself blush. Neil was staring straight at me and he was smirking a little bit. Jean, who was carefully trimming the massive eyebrows of Mr Ahmed, the school lollipop man, called over, 'Are you two OK, over there?'

'YEP,' we said.

'Good-oh,' she replied. 'Would you mind turning up the music a touch? It's so quiet in here that we're all in danger of falling asleep.'

I reached behind me and gladly turned up the volume control. Carole King's plonky piano playing filled the shop. There was now no possibility that my future mother-in-law Jean Stingecombe would be able to hear Neil's shameless sexual advances.

Neil raised his eyebrows at me and said, 'Well? What do you think?' He tapped the photo again and said, 'Would your Gareth be excited by something like this?'

I tried to picture Gareth with a Mohawk fin on his head. It was difficult though because Gareth's hair is quite fluffy and a bit awkward and tends to do its own thing. I shrugged my shoulders again and said, 'He might do.'

Neil said, 'Maybe I *should* then. If that's the look that the modern man is going for.' And then he winked at me. Neil is always winking at me.

Jean looked across at us and waved. Dilys had switched a hairdryer on and was giving Mrs John her weekly blow-dry. There was no possibility of being overheard. I decided that it was time to put Neil straight. In a low voice, I said, 'Look, Neil, you've gotta stop flirting like this because it's not appropriate in the workplace and, anyway, I'm just not interested. And if Jean hears you and tells Gareth, he'll go berserk.'

Neil looked startled for a moment and then he clapped his hand over his mouth and started laughing.

'It's not FUNNY,' I said, rather louder. 'I mean it. I know you've been out with every single girl in Whitchurch village but you're not going out with me because I'm already going out with Gaz.'

Neil stopped laughing and suddenly looked a bit upset. I shifted about on my stool, feeling awkward. 'I'm sorry, Neil,' I whispered. 'That's how it is. I'm just being honest with you.'

Neil went very red and very silent. For a couple of minutes, we sat looking at hair magazines and pretended to ignore each other. And then in a very low voice, he said, 'Can I be honest with *you* now, Lottie?'

'Yeah,' I said. 'But you'll have to speak up a bit because all I can hear is Carole King and her flipping piano. And Dilys's hairdryer isn't helping much either.'

But instead of speaking more loudly, Neil chewed his fingernails and murmured something in a voice no louder than a whisper.

I said, 'WHAT?'

Carole King wailed and plonked away on her piano. Jean Stingecombe chatted to Mr Ahmed. Dilys waved her hairdryer around.

With a red face, Neil said, 'Mumble mumble mumble.'

I said, 'HUH?'

Carole King carried on wailing and plonking. Jean shrieked with laughter at something that Mr Ahmed had said. Dilys turned her hairdryer up to a higher speed.

Neil said, 'I THINK –'

Carole King's song came to an end. Jean Stingecombe and Mr Ahmed lapsed into a momentary silence. Dilys switched off her hairdryer. Neil finished his sentence.

– ' I'M GAY!'

And then, realizing that everything around him had gone totally and utterly silent, he went very pale and looked as if he was about to be sick.

For a moment, the entire salon seemed to freeze and everyone was looking at Neil. But then the CD spun back into life and Carole King started singing another song. And Dilys laughed and shouted, 'Oooh, are you playing hard to get again, Neily?' And she waddled off to fetch the small mirror so that she could show Mrs John what the back of her head looked like.

Jean said, 'Watch him, Lottie! He's always playing games, that one.' And then she started asking Mr Ahmed about his hip-replacement operation.

I looked at Neil. I was feeling a bit weird. As if I'd just dreamed up the last couple of minutes in my head. I wasn't even sure that any of it had actually happened and was almost beginning to wonder if I'd just imagined the entire thing. But then Neil sighed and said, 'I keep trying to tell people. But nobody ever seems to listen.'

He leaned his elbows on the reception desk and put his head in his hands.

For a moment or two I sat and looked at him and didn't know what to say. And then, finally, I touched him on the arm and said the only thing I could think of to say and it was this:

'I'm listening, Neil.'

Neil lifted his head up and smiled at me and, with a look of total and utter relief, he said, 'Thanks, Lottie.' And I knew then that I'd actually said the right thing for once. And I didn't care one jot that he was gay. I was just glad that he'd finally found someone who would listen to him and I'm *still* really glad and surprised and proud to say that the listening person was me.

And the Third Shocking Revelation? Well, that came after the shop was closed. On the stroke of half past four, just as she had done on the two previous Saturdays, Jean clapped her hands together and said, 'It's staff development time, folks.' My heart sank and I looked over at Neil. It was *his* turn after all. But for once, Neil didn't seem to be in the mood. I suppose it's not every day of your life that you come out of the gay wardrobe. It must be very emotionally draining. I touched him on the elbow and said, 'It's all right, Neil. I'll do it.'

As I sat down, Jean said, 'I'm going to demonstrate curl and volume today. Lottie has got quite fine hair and clearly the light curl I added last Saturday wasn't enough because I couldn't help noticing that it was almost entirely gone by the time she came round to lunch on Sunday. So today, Lottie, we're going for more layering, more volume and more texture. It's going to look fantastic.' And then she began layering and volumizing and texturing my hair, and while she did, she sang the natural woman song and I sat very still with my fingers crossed and hoped and prayed that my hair would be OK.

When she'd finished, I looked at myself in the mirror. Only once. Very quickly. And then I shifted my gaze in another direction. It was very difficult to look myself in the eye. I looked like this:

My hair was actually even more putrid than last time.

'What do you think?' asked Jean.

'Hmm, it's good, hmmm,' I said in my best Pat Mumble voice, and then as soon as I possibly could, I got my bag, said bye to everyone and left.

I walked just as far as the traffic island and when I got there I plonked myself down on the bench and sat and stared at the passing cars. It was late in the day and there was hardly anyone else around. All the sixth-formers who use the island as their daily hang-out had cleared off and gone home and Elvis Presley – who uses it as his place to sleep – had woken up and gone to the pub[26]. Apart from the cars which kept whooshing by me, it felt almost as peaceful as it does inside my wardrobe. In fact, it felt so peaceful on that bench in the middle of Merthyr Road that, for a little while, I stopped worrying about my square hair and my non-existent physical relationship with Gareth Stingecombe and decided to DO SOMETHING POSITIVE. I pulled my phone out of my pocket and stared at it for ages. And then I pressed Goose's number. As I waited for my call to connect, a little voice in my head said, 'Don't give Goose a hard time.'

'I won't,' I said out loud. I meant it as well. I wanted to sort this whole stupid argument out once and for all. I wanted us to be best friends again.

A voice on the other end of my phone said, 'Hi, Lottie.' It wasn't Goose's voice. But it was definitely a familiar voice.

'Goose?' I said.

---

[26] Probably.

'No,' said the familiar voice. 'Goose has just popped downstairs to talk to her mum. Can I give her a message?'

'Who is this?' I said.

'It's Samantha. Me and Goose were just talking in her bedroom and her mum –'

'You're around Goose's house?' I said.

'Well . . . yeah,' said Samantha Morgan.

'Oh great!' I said. And all of a sudden, I stopped feeling peaceful and positive and just felt fantastically peeved instead.

'Look, Lottie, I'm not trying to cause any trouble between—'

'Oh, whatever,' I said. 'I really don't care.' And then I switched my phone off.

I did care though because I sat on the bench for another twenty minutes and muttered to myself. And then, just as I was starting to run out of things to mutter about, I spotted Neil Adam striding towards me in his leopard-print raincoat and he was waving at me. In spite of the fact that I was fantastically peeved off, I couldn't help smiling because not so long ago, I'd have been completely over-excited by the mere possibility that the stunningly sexadelic Neil Adam would ever want to wave at ME. But the funny thing is that even though I don't fancy him any more, I actually like him much better than I ever used to.

'All right, Neil?' I said.

Neil sat down next to me on the bench and said, 'I just wanted to say thanks again for being so cool today.'

Even though I was fantastically peeved off, I smiled and said, 'It's all right.'

'Yeah, well, I appreciate it,' he said and then he gave me a sudden peck on the cheek and got up and began to walk right back up the street again.

'Hey, Neil,' I said, calling after him.

He stopped and looked back at me.

'Be honest with me, has Jean given me square hair?' I asked.

Neil pulled a sympathetic face. 'To be fair, I suppose she has, yeah.'

I sighed and nodded. Then I asked, 'Does she do staff development *every* Saturday?'

Neil nodded. 'It's all part of the job, I'm afraid, Lottie.'

And that was when I experienced my Third Shocking Revelation. It hit the top of my head like a thunderbolt. 'Thanks,' I said. 'You look after yourself, now.'

Neil frowned. 'You're gonna quit the salon, aren't you?'

I nodded again. 'I've got to, Neil. It's too stressful. I can't cope with hair like this every weekend. The money's handy but I'm not desperate. I'll see you around though, yeah?' Then I got up, lowered my square head and walked home really fast.

And although I'm generally quite a sociable person, I'm actually relieved that I've been forced to spend this particular Saturday evening on my own. Except for the Emotion Notepad and Winnie, of course. And they couldn't care less what my hair looks like.

hOw I GLImPseD the LIGht whILe I was IN the Dark

Normally I don't like Sundays. Sundays have a tendency to bore me into oblivion. In Whitchurch, all the shops and cafes are shut and there's never anything much to do other than sit in the public garden or hang out at the bus shelter. And even if I stay indoors, I end up getting bored to tears. My mum tries to force me to do a bit of the housework, and when that fails, she nags me to do my homework and usually I just go upstairs and do it because I might as well, seeing as how there's nothing else to do. On Sundays, even the TV isn't worth watching. Unless you like watching programmes about gardening or God, that is. Or *Antiques Roadshow*.

But today hasn't been like that. Today has been brilliant and momentous and extremely enlightening. Because I had a visitor.

It was just after lunch and I was sitting in my bedroom playing with Winnie when, downstairs, the doorbell rang. I picked up Winnie and, holding him close to me so he couldn't make a bouncy escape, I sneaked out on to the landing to find out who the visitor was. I didn't expect for one second that it was anybody who wanted to see me. Gareth had already told me that he'd be at his nan's house all day and, apart from him, nobody has called round to see me in ages. Not even my dad.

Downstairs, I heard my mum say, 'Hello, stranger! How

lovely to see you!' I frowned and edged a little closer to the top of the stairs. Whoever it was, it definitely wasn't my dad! My mum is never pleased to see him. I edged closer still. My mum, unaware that I was listening just above her head, shouted up, 'Lottie! Can you come down, please? Goose is here.'

For a moment, I froze on the landing with Winnie still hugged against me. And then I darted back into my bedroom, shoved Winnie into his cage and did the only thing that I could think of to do. I climbed inside my wardrobe and shut the door.

Don't think I didn't want to see Goose. Because I did. I REALLY REALLY did. Gareth Stingecombe is a fantastic person but he's useless at talking shoes. Or hair dye. And I can't have races with him to see which of us can eat a family bag of marshmallows the fastest because it's just not the sort of thing you do when you're trying to look sexy. So he definitely has his place in my life but in no way is he a replacement for Goose. But as happy as I was that she'd called round to see me, I was also feeling seriously freaked out. I had this colossal fear that, somehow, I'd say the wrong thing and make things between us *even* more terrible than they already were. I suppose it's fair to say that I was experiencing a few confidence issues. It's hardly surprising though. Just recently, whenever I've tried to talk to Goose, we've ended up practically fighting. This tells me something interesting about my peacemaking skills. It tells me I haven't got any.

From inside my wardrobe, I heard my mum barge her

way into my bedroom and say, 'Lottie, Goose is . . . oh!'
And then there was a sudden silence.

I hugged my knees and held my breath and hoped my
mum would clear off.

After a moment or two, my mum knocked on the
wardrobe door.

'Go away!' I said.

On the other side of the wardrobe door, there was a deep
sigh. Then my mum said, 'I don't know what the problem
is between you two but Goose has made the effort to come
round so you can make the effort to get out of that wardrobe
and talk to her. Surely you can manage that much?' She
sounded a bit cross.

'I doubt it!' I said. I was feeling a bit cross too.

There was another short pause and then my mum said,
'In that case, I'll send her up here.'

'YOU WILL NOT!' I said.

'Watch me!' said my mum. She was really getting on my
nerves. Even so, with the benefit of hindsight, I wouldn't
swap her for a different mum.

Outside, everything went quiet and I guessed that my
mum had gone downstairs and was telling Goose to come
on up. I bit my thumbnail anxiously and quickly tried to
take stock of the situation. I'd never discussed my wardrobe
habit with Goose. I had no idea how she was going to react.
From another person's point of view, I admit that it can
seem quite weird. With this thought in mind, I was just
about to clamber out when I heard the door of my bedroom

creak open. Instantly, I sat back down and huddled myself up tighter. If there's one thing that looks more mad and undignified than being caught sitting in your own wardrobe, it's probably being caught clambering out of it.

Goose said, 'Lottie?'

I hugged my knees and held my breath and hoped she would go away.

In a confused voice, Goose said, 'Er . . . I thought your mum was joking when she said you might be in the wardrobe.'

Inside the wardrobe, I sighed and said, 'Well, guess what? She wasn't.'

Outside the wardrobe, Goose said, 'So are you coming out then?'

'I doubt it,' I said.

There was a short pause and then Goose said, 'Oh well, I suppose there's only one thing for me to do then, isn't there?'

Before I had a chance to reply, the door of my wardrobe opened and Goose said, 'Budge up!' And the next thing I knew, she had squeezed in and was sitting huddled up beside me in my wardrobe.

We must have looked like this.

After a little while, I said, 'This is a bit weird, isn't it?'

Goose said, 'Oh, I don't know, I quite like it in here. It is a bit fusty though.'

'It's OK when it's your own fust,' I said.

Goose said, 'Hmmm. Perhaps.'

For a few minutes, we sat huddled side by side and silently adjusted to each other's presence. I'm not used to sharing my wardrobe. I chewed my thumbnail again and hoped that Goose would speak first because I was feeling a bit uncomfortable and awkward and couldn't think of a single thing to say. But next to me, Goose just sat in the dark and said nothing and the silence seemed to get thicker and thicker. I suppose she must have been feeling a bit awkward too. To be fair to her, she's probably not used to conducting conversations from within a wardrobe. Neither am I, really.

I racked my brains for a conversational opener and,

eventually, something popped into my head. I said, '*Beth sy'n cwcan yn dy bopty poeth gwyllt, cariad?*'

In the darkness, Goose chuckled and said, '*Dim lot!*'[27]

And then I said, 'So what brings you to my wardrobe?'

Goose said, 'I miss you, Lotts.'

In the darkness, I smiled. I could tell that Goose was smiling too because I'd heard it in her voice. You don't have to see a smile to know it's there. You can hear them too. You can't smell them though. After a moment or two, I said, 'I miss you lots too.'

Goose gave a shrug. She was so close to me, I was able to feel it. 'It's been totally tragic without you around. I haven't timed how fast I can eat a family bag of marshmallows for ages and I can't actually remember the last time I had a decent discussion about shoes.' She sighed again. 'Even the *Free Willy* films seem a bit pathetic when you watch them on your own.'

'I thought you just wanted to hang around with Samantha Morgan,' I said. 'And Spud.'

Goose was quiet for a moment. And then she said, 'I like Sam. She told me all about what happened in Year 9 and she feels bad about it. And she only came round my house yesterday to tell me about what happened with Lee Fogel. She thinks you and me should be friends again.'

This time, I was quiet. Finally, I said, 'Do *you* think we

---

[27] This means 'Not much!' in Welsh. I'm not going to explain all over again what my question meant because I've already explained it in footnote 23.

should be friends again?' I'm not really sure why I even asked this because I was already pretty sure I knew the answer.

In her best Kentucky accent, Goose said, 'Well, hey, I guess, Jonice.' And then in her normal voice, she added, 'Of course I do. You're the best friend I've ever had.'

In my best Kentucky accent, I said, 'Well, hey, Janice, that's swell.' And then in my normal voice, I took a great big deep breath and said, 'I'm sorry if I've been acting a bit self-obsessed recently. Sometimes the inside of my head is all me me me.'

In the fusty darkness of my wardrobe, Goose gave an awkward cough. 'I just thought that you'd got so carried away with Stingecombe that you couldn't be bothered with me any more.' She sniffed and then added, 'You haven't phoned me or called round for me or even bothered to walk to school with me for ages.'

We lapsed into silence again and then, after what felt like another eternity, I said, 'Sorry.'

In the darkness, Goose fumbled for my hand and squeezed it. 'It's all right,' she said.

It was nice just sitting there in the dark with Goose. It was nice to have her back again. She's the best friend I've ever had and I reckon we'll still be hanging out together when we're eighty. I racked my brains for something else to say. Finally, I said, 'Did you know that Neil Adam is gay?'

'WHAT?' In the cramped space of my wardrobe, I sensed Goose's entire body stiffen in shock. For a moment she even stopped breathing, and then she said, 'Mad Alien? Are you sure?'

'Yep,' I said. 'He told me so himself.' And then, suddenly feeling a bit terrible, I added, 'But don't tell anyone else though. I don't think he's ready to go public yet.'

'OH . . . MY . . . GOD!' said Goose. 'I used to go out with him! I'VE SNOGGED HIM LOADS OF TIMES!' In a whisper, she added, 'Does that mean I'm bisexual?'

I burst out laughing. For someone who is really clever, Goose can actually be incredibly stupid sometimes. 'Don't be daft,' I said. 'It's not like a cold. You can't catch it off him.'

Goose went quiet for a moment and then she said, 'I suppose that *was* a bit daft but it's just a bit of a shock, that's all.'

Even though she could barely see me, I nodded sympathetically. 'I know. I was a bit shocked too when he told me. But the more I think about it, the more it all seems to make sense really. I'm glad he told me.'

There was another long pause and then I cleared my throat and said, 'Goose, can I ask you something?'

'Sure.'

'Have you done *it* with Spud?' Even though we were protected by the privacy of my wardrobe, I decided to whisper this just in case my mum was sitting on the other side of the door with an undercover surveillance secret listening device. You can never be too careful. Not when your mum is a police sergeant in the South Wales Police.

Goose said, 'What? *It?*'

'Yeah,' I said.

There was a silence. Then Goose said, 'You mean the Grand Slam?'

'Yeah,' I said.

'The Full Monty?' said Goose.

'Yeah,' I said.

'The Humpty Dumpty?'

'Yeah,' I said.

Then she went quiet for a moment.

'No.'

In the darkness, my mouth fell open with surprise. 'Really?'

'Really,' said Goose. 'I don't fancy that yet. Spud is really nice and everything but I'm not so desperate that I'm ready to give away my gold to him. He's only sixteen. Anything could happen to him. What if he turns out to be a total numpty or something? I might regret it forever.'

For someone who is incredibly stupid sometimes, Goose can be extremely wise. I frowned and then, in a slightly tetchy tone, I said, 'But you let him give you a colossal great love bite.'

'Yeah,' said Goose, 'but I wasn't too chuffed when I saw how blinking hideous it looked. He won't be doing that again in a hurry because I told him he'll get dumped if he does.'

'Oh,' I said and frowned again.

'Have *you* done *it*?' asked Goose.

I fiddled with the lace of my trainer and felt myself blush.

Then I said, 'No, but Gareth and I have discussed it and we're probably going to do *it* on Tuesday when his parents are out line dancing.'

'REALLY?' said Goose. Even though it was dark, I could tell that Goose's eyes had gone really wide because I could just about make out the white bits. She looked like this:

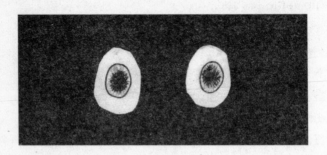

After another pause, she said, 'Do you *want* to?

And this is where it gets totally weird. Because ever since I saw Gareth in those Britney Spears boxer shorts I've been unable to think of anything else EXCEPT wanting to, but all of a sudden, right then and there in the inner calm of my wardrobe, I wasn't exactly sure any more if I actually *did* want to. I'm not desperate, you know.

Goose must have noticed my silence because she said, 'Gareth's not putting pressure on you, is he?'

'NO!' I said. 'NO WAY IS HE! In fact, it's Gaz and his busy rugby schedule causing all the delay.'

'But he *does* want to do it, doesn't he?' said Goose.

'He's fifteen and he's male,' I said. 'Of course he does!' And then, all of a sudden, my mouth dropped open in shock and a blinding light of revelation was abruptly switched on in my dull brain. It was just as if somebody had walloped me over the head with a sledgehammer. But before I could say anything more to Goose, I heard a noise outside. 'Shh,' I said. We both fell silent and listened as my bedroom door creaked open. Then we heard my mum say, 'I've brought you up some tea and some . . .' Her voice trailed off into silence.

Goose giggled.

'We're in here,' I said.

'What? *Both* of you?' said my mum.

'Yep,' I said.

'Hi,' shouted Goose.

My mum made a huffy-puffy noise and I heard the sound of a tray being placed on my desk. 'Suit yourselves,' said my mum and then she went back downstairs.

I pushed open the wardrobe door. 'My mum's brought us some cake,' I said. I inched forward on my knees and then clambered out of the wardrobe. 'Come on, Goose,' I said. 'It's a bit too cramped in there for two of us.'

Goose clambered out behind me and then, back in the real world, she blinked her eyes and frowned. 'What's happened to your hair?' she asked.

'Gareth's mum did it,' I said. 'I've been working at her salon and she keeps trying things out on my hair.'

Goose eyed my layered, textured and volumized hair suspiciously. 'You'll have to leave,' she said.

I nodded in agreement. 'Don't worry, I'm going to.'

We sat on the floor of my bedroom eating cake. Goose waved at Winnie and said, 'I haven't actually even met your chinchilla yet. He looks a bit old.'

'He's ancient,' I said proudly. 'But he's totally lush. I love him.'

Goose looked at Winnie enviously. 'I wish I had one.'

I shrugged. 'They're terrible at night though. I haven't had a decent night's kip since I got him.'

Goose put her cake down, confused. 'Why don't you just put his cage in another room?'

I looked at Goose. Then I looked at Winnie. And then, almost unable to believe how colossally thick I've been, I said, 'Oh yeah!'

Goose said, 'Hey, I nearly forgot. I've brought you a present. A sort of peace offering.' She leaned over and reached for her bag. Then she pulled something out of it and handed it to me. It was a CD.

I took it and looked at it. There was a hippy woman and a cat on the cover.

I stared at the CD in disbelief and said, 'Is this a joke?'

Goose's cheeks went purple. 'No,' she said. 'I love that album! My dad plays it all the time. Did you know that Carole King's *Tapestry* is the thirty-sixth greatest album ever made? Honestly, Lottie, you should listen to it. It's got some really sweet songs on it.'

I could tell my reaction had upset her a bit. Quickly, I said, 'I didn't mean to sound ungrateful. It's just that Gareth's mum plays this *all the time* in the hair salon. But thank you.'

Goose said, 'I wanted to give you this because I've been feeling so bad about all those terrible things I said to you on the phone the other day – not to mention the catty comments we made to each other in English via that Oscar Wilde book.'

I bit my lip. Me and Goose have been quite horrible to each other in English recently.

Goose continued, 'I think Oscar Wilde is a good writer and everything but I don't necessarily think he's as incredibly wise as Mr Wood thinks he is. I can imagine he might have been a bit annoying if you actually knew him.' She tapped the CD which was still in my hand. 'Whereas Carole King *really* knows what she's talking about. There's a song on here called 'You've Got a Friend'. I wish *I'd* written that song – and I'd have written it for you.' And then, with no warning whatsoever, she threw her arms around me and gave me a massive tight hug and I actually almost very nearly started to cry because I realized then that I am one of the luckiest fifteen-year-olds in Cardiff. If not the whole world.

aND hOw Gareth stINGeCOmBe Gave me a QuICk POke whILe hIs PareNts were LINe DaNCING

I am an astronaut surfing a wave on the Sea of Tranquillity. I have driven too fast down the motorway to Misery, sailed too far on the sinking ship to Stress and almost lost my head on the bullet train to Oblivion. But that's all in the past. What really matters is *now*. And right now, I'm feeling utterly fantastic. Because I've kept my balance and surfed my way to the calmest coastline in the galaxy.

And Gareth Stingecombe is waiting on the dusty moon beach to meet me . . .

Or rather, he's not on the dusty moon beach, he's in his house. And he's opening the front door to me and standing to one side so I can come in from the street. And instead of a surfboard, I am carrying two portions of sausage and chips all wrapped up in newspaper. And instead of a spacesuit, Gareth is wearing his smartest jeans and a U2 T-shirt. I don't really like U2 but he still looks sexadelic.

'All right, Gaz?' I say.

'Pretty good,' he says.

'I've brought us sausage and chips,' I say.

'Cracking!' he says. And then he looks apologetic and adds, 'So my mum has messed your hair up again?'

'Mmm,' I say. I glance around the hallway and, ever so casually, I ask, 'So your mum and dad have gone line dancing, have they?'

'Mmm,' says Gareth and he looks a bit embarrassed.

I follow him through to the living room and we both perch on the edge of the big sofa and unwrap the parcels of food.

Gareth Stingecombe is quieter than usual. He picks up the remote control and turns on the television. A programme about cooking appears on the screen and Gareth leaves it there and pretends that he's watching it. I can tell he's got something on his mind. I've got something on my mind too. Mostly it's this:

Sometimes I can be a bit **NAIVE**

And in the very back of my head, I've also got this niggling feeling that I can be a bit selfish too at times.

I stare down at my food and try to think of something to say which will make things easier. But nothing comes to me. Sighing, I spear my sausage with my white plastic fork and, nudging Gareth, I say, 'It seemed a good idea at the time but I'm not really in the mood for a sausage now, Gaz.'

Gareth stares at me and his cheeks go red. He looks at the sausage and then he looks at me and then, nervously, he clears his throat. 'The thing is, Lottie,' he says, 'at the end of the day – looking at it from every available angle – when all is said and done – I just don't think I'm ready.' He goes even redder and stares down at the floor. 'I don't care what anyone else thinks. I really like you, Lottie, and I don't want to mess things up by rushing into anything.' And then he takes a deep breath and just shrugs.

My cheeks have gone very red too. I know they have because they feel hot enough to fry a couple of eggs on. To be honest, I'm not really surprised by what Gareth has just said. At some point when I was in my wardrobe, I think I worked it out for myself. I suppose you could say that I'm finally learning how to see things from a different angle. Carefully, I put my chips on to the coffee table and then I bite my thumbnail for a moment. In a very small voice, I say, 'Actually, I'm not ready either.'

For a moment, Gareth stares at me in disbelief and then, slowly, a little smile starts to spread over his lovely face. Relief floods over me. In fact, I feel as relieved as the most relieved person in the whole of Relieved-Land. I give Gareth a little smile back and then, because I know I've been a bit of a numpty, I whisper the word, 'Sorry.'

Gareth's smile breaks out into a big grin. I grin back at him. Then I remember something. I reach into my pocket and pull out a folded piece of paper which I hand to him. Gareth's forehead crumples in an expression of puzzlement and he takes the paper from me and reads it. It is the sonnet I wrote the other week when I wasn't able to sleep. I hold my breath and cross my fingers, hoping desperately that he won't think I'm a stalker. Finally, he says, 'Do you know what? You rock my world, Lottie Biggs.' And then he gives me a quick poke in the ribs. Not hard. Just friendly.

And if I had a pause button which could freeze me forever at one specific moment in time, I'd have definitely pressed it right then. But I haven't. So instead, I'm sitting in my bedroom and living the whole scene all over again in my head as I tap away on my computer. In the background, the Carole King CD that Goose gave me is softly playing and I'm really *really* starting to like it. And there's nothing more I can think of to say right now other than THAT was how Gareth Stingecombe made me feel like a natural woman!

haYLeY LONG has a MassIve LIst Of thaNk YOUs, startING wIth:

haYLeY YeeLes, mY aGeNt, whO has LOaDs Of GOOD IDeas aND aLwaYs seNDs me CheerY eMaILs; emMa, ruth aND raCheL at MaCMILLaN fOr aLL theIr heLP aND LOveLY LuNChes; LaUreN reeves, mY haIrDresser, fOr teLLING me aLL her fuNNY haIrDressING stOrIes; CarOLe BUrtON aND MeLaNIe westLake fOr taLkING tO me aBOut COGNItIve BehavIOUraL theraPY aND stuff; meL aND sCOtt thOMas fOr BeING mY hOtLINe tO sCIeNtIfIC wIsDOm; GweN DavIes fOr BeING mY weLsh LaNGuaGe eXPert aND aLsO fOr LeNDING me her tOtaLLY LUsh CaravaN; sweeeet INkY MOLe fOr DrawING the GrOOvY COvers, aND PastON COLLeGe, NOrfOLk BeCause I tOtaLLY LOve It there.

aND Gt as aLwaYs XXX

aBOut the authOr

haYLeY LONG was born in Ipswich ages ago. She studied English at university in Wales, where she had a very nice time and didn't do much work. After that she spent several years in various places abroad and had a very nice time and didn't do much work then either. Now **haYLeY** is an English **teaCher** and works very hard indeed. She lives in Norwich with a **raBBIt** called **Irma** and a **husBaND**. The Lottie books are her first for young adults – and there will be more from **LOttIe** (and **haYLeY**) **COmING sOON.**

if, Like LOttie, YOu fiND YOurseLf wONDeriNG
what Life is aLL aBOut, there are LOts
Of weBsites aND PeOPLe YOu CaN CaLL tO fiND
Out mOre aBOut hOw YOu are feeLiNG:

www.**teeNisssues**.co.uk

www.**saNe**.OrG.uk
☎ **08457 67 80 00**

www.**ChaNNeL4**.cOm/heaLth/miCrOsites/0-9/4heaLth/teeNLife/

samarItaNs – PrOviDiNG 24-hOur
CONfiDeNtiaL emOtiONaL suPPOrt fOr PeOPLe iN NeeD
☎ **08457 90 90 90**

suPPOrtLiNe – PrOviDiNG CONfiDeNtiaL
emOtiONaL suPPOrt iN PartiCuLar fOr ChiLDreN aND YOuNG aDuLts
ON a varietY Of issues iNCLuDiNG stress, DePressiON aND aNXietY
☎ **020 8554 9004**

Or YOu CaN aLwaYs taLk tO sOmeONe
CLOse tO YOu:
YOur famiLY, a frieND, a DOCtOr, a teaCher –
it wOrkeD fOr LOttie iN **the eND!**

Do you use your own experiences in your books?

Yes, all the time. Actually almost everything I write about is either inspired by something which has happened to me or something which I've heard about from someone else. I couldn't possibly write some off-the-wall fantasy novel because I don't think I'm imaginative enough. But I do have a really good memory for collecting strange useless pieces of information – stuff like funny things I've heard people say, song lyrics, weird objects . . . they all seem to get stuck in my brain forever. I can remember a talking doll I had when I was about five and every single weird thing she said. So I put that doll into the first Lottie Biggs book.

Then there are bigger experiences like how I worked in a shoe shop on Saturdays when I was a teenager and even how I started to feel really miserable a while back. Obviously that wasn't a good state to be in, but by writing Lottie Biggs it helped me to make something worthwhile out of even that rubbish time.

Having said that, I'm definitely not Lottie Biggs, and what I write is always fiction and not autobiography. Lottie would be a lot more boring if she merely represented me at fifteen. She wouldn't have a lush boyfriend like Gareth for a start!

Did you think you had a chance of becoming an author?

Um, I never really thought about the end result of actually being an author. To be honest, I don't really think of myself in that way even now. If anyone asks me what I do, I usually say that I'm a teacher. I find it easier! But I've always wanted to write novels since I was in primary school. When I was about eight, I even typed one up on my mum's typewriter and sent it to a publisher. In my head, it always seemed to be a question of when I get published, rather than if. But that's because I was always writing something.

Who inspired you to write?

That's difficult. I'm not sure really. In my family nobody other than me was a big reader and certainly nobody else ever wrote anything down just for the fun of it. But I've always been reading books. When I was really young, my mum used to make me put my book down and go out to play more with the other kids in my road because otherwise I would have just stayed indoors all the time. I don't know where I got that reading habit from. But I suppose I should thank Enid Blyton really. Although her books are not really fashionable now, I read hundreds of them when I was a child. So perhaps it was her who made me want to tell stories of my own.

Are there any recent books that you admire?

Well it's quite a few years old now but *Holes* by Louis Sachar is one of my favourite ever books and definitely my favourite book for young people. In fact, it was reading that book a few years ago which encouraged me to write for a younger audience. Until then, I'd only ever written for adults. I haven't read anything to topple *Holes* from my number-one spot. I do read some teen fiction, but I try to avoid anything which looks remotely like what I'm writing. I wouldn't want it to influence how I write. Some readers have suggested that I've adopted the style of Louise Rennison. I take this as a compliment because she is hugely successful, but the truth is – I haven't actually read any of her titles.

I know that books about vampires are very popular at the moment and I did give a couple of these a go but didn't really get on with them. However, there is a book called *The Historian* by Elizabeth Kostova that came out a few years ago which is absolutely stunning. It's very exciting, very frightening and very intelligent. I definitely admire that book.

Interview by Sasha, reproduced with kind permission of the utterly fantastic Chicklish website: www.chicklish.co.uk

Lottie Biggs is NOT Mad

HayleyLong

am I JeaLOus that mY Best frieND has
a **BOYfrieND**? DOes that meaN I'm
traGIC??? Is mY CurreNt haIr COLOur
(meLODY DeeP PLum) Better thaN that
DODGY CustarD COLOur I trIeD Last week?

PerhaPs I **ShOuLD** GO Out wIth
Gareth stINGeCOmBe — eveN thOuGh I DON't
faNCY hIm the Least tINIest BIt.
If I DON't faNCY Gareth stINGeCOmBe the
Least tINIest BIt, whY am I OBsessING
aBOut hIs maNLY thINGs?

thIs Is a BOOk aBOut aLL the ImPOrtaNt
QuestIONs IN LIfe. It's DefINIteLY **NOt**
aBOut sIttING IN mY warDrOBe Or havING
a meNtaL DIsturBaNCe Of aNY kIND . . .

Finding Cassie Crazy

Jaclyn Moriarty

Dear Beautiful,

You're making me nervous by being so weird.

But your weirdness is what I like about you . . .

The Ashbury–Brookfield Pen-Pal Project starts out as one annoying English teacher's desire to bring back the art of letter-writing, but for best friends Em, Lydia and Cassie, writing to complete strangers who happen to be 'Brooker Boys' has a seriously surprising outcome.

While Emily and Lydia are busy flirting, fragile Cass has to cope with a boy who seems to hate her. It's just one more problem on a long list, but when her friends find out, full-on war between the schools is inevitable . . .

A selected list of titles available from Macmillan Children's Books

The prices shown below are correct at the time of going to press. However, Macmillan Publishers reserves the right to show new retail prices on covers, which may differ from those previously advertised.

All Pan Macmillan titles can be ordered from our website, www.panmacmillan.com, or from your local bookshop and are also available by post from:

Bookpost, PO Box 29, Douglas, Isle of Man IM99 1BQ

Credit cards accepted. For details:
Telephone: 01624 677237
Fax: 01624 670923
Email: bookshop@enterprise.net
www.bookpost.co.uk

Free postage and packing in the United Kingdom